GW00703208

DAYS OF OUR LIVES...

CREATIVE WRITING FROM HOME COUNTIES SOUTH

Edited by Heather Killingray

First published in Great Britain in 2002 by
YOUNG WRITERS
Remus House,
Coltsfoot Drive,
Peterborough, PE2 9JX
Telephone (01733) 890066

All Rights Reserved

Copyright Contributors 2002

HB ISBN 0 75432 756 6
SB ISBN 0 75432 757 4

FOREWORD

This year Young Writers proudly presents a showcase of the best 'Days Of Our Lives . . .' short stories, from up-and-coming writers nationwide.

To write a short story is a difficult exercise. We made it more challenging by setting the theme of 'A Day In The Life Of Someone From The Second Millennium', using no more than 250 words! Much imagination and skill is required. *Days Of Our Lives . . . Creative Writing From Home Counties South* achieves and exceeds these requirements. This exciting anthology will not disappoint the reader.

The thought, effort, imagination and hard work put into each story impressed us all, and again, the task of editing proved demanding due to the quality of entries received, but was nevertheless enjoyable.

We hope you are as pleased as we are with the final selection and that you continue to enjoy *Days Of Our Lives . . . Creative Writing From Home Counties South* for many years to come.

CONTENTS

Alexis Ellender	88
Isobel Wright	89
Sathia Narayana Navaneetham	90
Javed Ahmed	92
Christopher Newton	93
Oliver Piested	94
Ben Rivans	95
Sameera Yasin	96
Robert Gholam	98
Jamie Walker	100
Liam Berger	101
Caryl Morgan	102

Madley Primary School

Ashley Morgan	103
Robyn Barratt	104
Sarah Guy	105
Emma Butler	106
Matthew Hancox	107
Matthew Jones	108
Alexandra Bolton	109
Alexander Fraser	110

Morgans Primary School

David Newstead	111
Tobi Martin	113
Michael Dunnage	114
William Brady	116
Elliot Rogers	118
Jack Stingemore	119
James Robinson	120
Thayla Banks	121
Jasmine Cowler	122
Emily Wheeler	123
Emily Unwin	124
Danielle Leber	126

Caine Marshall	200
Oliver Baum	201
Rebecca Shaw	202
Louise Peppis-Whalley	203
Sean Julliard	204
Tristan Loffler	205
Carly Clarke	206
Christopher McLaughlin	207
Pablo Shah	208
Anel Kahrimanovic	209
Jonathan Littledale	210
Louis Archer	211
Kaori Takenaka	212
Alex Dehnel	213
David Fairbairn	214
Hayley Gardiner	215
Max Effendowicz	216
Jack Schofield	217
Scott Jermy	218
Edward Allinson	219
Alice Wilson	220
Edmund Croall	221

Stapleford Primary School
Tom Ashby	222

Town Farm Primary School
Samantha Harris	223
Catherine Lesley	224
Douglas Clayton	225
Samuel Chesterman	226
Jack Banks	227
Shauna Giddens	228
Danny Hadley	229
Jack Woods	230
Zahid Zafar	231
Lisa Stevens	232

The Stories

THE TREE THAT SAVED MY LIFE

It was a cold and windy morning although the season was summer. As I was walking along the soft verdant grass, I heard a dog barking. Then suddenly I found myself running very fast. The dog was chasing me. There was a tree in the field. I ran up to it and hid in a hole so the dog would not get me. I was very thirsty but when it started to rain I drank some water from the silky leaves.

After a while I began to feel hungry and for food I ate the nuts on the tree. The juicy white nut inside was an enjoyable sweet taste. This tree was a very welcome home for me, I really love it because it gave me food and water and saved my life.

It became night and it was cold. Then another squirrel came. But then I knew I had fallen in love with him and so did he with me. There we sat in the pitch-black night. The cold never hit us, our love made us warm.

That tree saved my life and made me a happier person. Just a tree, by itself, on its own. Just a tree made me have a lovely life like I had never had. Now I have got seven children thanks to the tree because it saved my children's lives by giving them food and water.

Esra Dokgöz (11)
Bonneygrove Primary School

THE DAY I WAS MY PARROT

I wake up, my eyes opened slowly like a tortoise just about to walk. I look around and around as if I have an owl's head. I see lots of things, like a bird in the air. I see the bright sofa, red like an apple, a huge black TV, a luminous green CD player and the long poles on my cage. The poles are like a giraffe's neck, they are gold like water and sun meeting.

The front door opens, it creaks, the floorboards rumble. It is my fantastic, careful owner. He walks over and opens my superb cage that he bought me. I flap my wonderful wing and fly around in the kitchen. Whilst flying, I take one cookie at a time. The white fridge is like a polar bear. My wings are as colourful as Elmer the elephant (on the book) superb!

My owner gets my water from the fridge, so it is nice and cold. My food comes from the cupboard in a huge round tube. My water is hooked to my cage and I can get my water from there. My life is the best. Superb! Fantastic!

Billy Langford (11)
Bonneygrove Primary School

DOLPHIN SAVES BOY'S LIFE

One summer as I was swimming on my own I looked up into the sky and saw a lovely colourful bird flying to get some food for its little ones.

After a while I started getting hungry when I saw a boy coming along with a bucket of fish. The next minute I saw the boy throwing fish into the water for me to eat. The boy started to play with me and we became friends. Every day he came to visit me at the swimming pool.

The next morning when the boy came to visit me he was throwing a ball at me because he wanted to play with me. After ten minutes he came next to me and started rubbing my head.

When he stepped to sit down on the stairs, he fell into the water and could not swim. When I could not see where the boy was I looked in the water and saw that the boy could not come up to the top. I came to save him. When the boy stopped breathing, I quickly put him on my back and took him and put him on the side of the swimming pool. I put my mouth on his tummy and started hitting him. Thanks to me the boy's life was saved. Now he was alright. the next day the boy asked his mum and dad if he could buy the dolphin. His mum and dad said
'Yes, on condition you feed it every day.'

Rain Bomboz (11)
Bonneygrove Primary School

A VERY SPECIAL PUPPY

One sunny bright morning, I woke up. It was my birthday. I only had one present. I opened it and I was amazed by the sight of it. It was a puppy a Dalmatian. I called it Spotty. It goes for five walks every day and it enjoys living with me.

Two months on, puppy's point of view.

I awoke, startled, ran on to my owner's bed, breathed in and really loudly barked and it got him out of bed. I ran like a rocket to fetch my pretty lead. I gave it to my owner as he was saying,
'Mum I'm taking the puppy out!'
So he opened the door and that was when the fun started. I also chased the cats which was also fun.

At 5.00pm, I had my lovely, delicious Pedigree dinner. After that at 6.30pm I had my fifth walk and we played ball at the same time. That walk was five miles long.

At 7.35pm I got stroked for five minutes, which sent me to sleep. That is one whole day for me in my lovely home.

Elliott Crighton Grant (11)
Bonneygrove Primary School

THE TREE

They are back. I thought yesterday was the last day, but no, here they are. I can hear them sawing in the distance, see each tree fall down with an almighty crash. I feel afraid. I know it is only days until they reach me. I am still quite young and still have a lot more sunsets to see.

It is not only the people in the distance, it's also the hunters. They come into my woods shooting all in their paths and, with the enormous guns, the poor animals do not have a chance. They have already killed hundreds. The walkers are not so innocent coming into my wood with dogs and children and littering my beautiful forest.

A storm came up this morning, it blew the leaves right off me. The ground was covered in glowing green leaves, but the sun is shining now and I feel great but I do not think that it will last long, for the cutters are moving in.

I can see them now, each tree falls and they show no mercy. What happens when they reach me? They are right near me now, I am so scared. I do not want to die. They are standing in front of me now. I cannot hear what they are saying but one of the men has taken a knife out. I hope I am turned into something useful when I am gone.

Leanne Mevo (11)
Bonneygrove Primary School

A DAY IN THE LIFE OF MY FOUNTAIN PEN

When I woke up this morning, I felt rather strange, and I still do! I feel rigid and, well cylinderish. It is pitch-black at the moment, there is a sort of other cylinder over my head. Hold on a minute, I'm moving!

That journey took a little while but now I'm not moving anymore, someone has taken the cylinder off my head and now I can see perfectly, that's not right, why am I in my classroom? Hey stop that, they keep pressing my head against paper. That cannot be right . . . oh my goodness, I'm a pen!

Later that day after I had made friends with the very nice pencil rubber and pencil sharpener that lived in the pencil case, I was passed by my owner to another child. This child used me for five minutes and then left me carelessly on his desk. Thirty seconds later, I accidentally rolled off and lay forgotten on the floor. I could see my owner searching for me, I called out to him but he could not hear me. Then a lovely little girl found me and handed me back to my owner. There was another journey in the pencil case which I was sure was the journey home and then I fell asleep hoping that I would be back to normal in the morning. When I woke up I felt all bendy and rubbery and I had a strange urge to erase something . . .

Georgia Hewlett (11)
Bonneygrove Primary School

WHEN I WAS A DOG

I awoke on Monday feeling different than normal, as I opened my eyes I gasped in surprise, there was a girl in my bed! Only I was not in my bed, I was in a total stranger's bed! I jumped off the bed to find something tall following me, I turned round to see that the 'thing' had a brownish body which was attached to me!

I ran to the bathroom mirror, only to find I was too small to see into it, I also had paws, I was a dog!

Immediately I panicked, where was I? How did I get here? How long would I be here?

'Nicky, where are you Nicky?' called the girl.
Slowly I edged towards the door and barked softly.

Knock, knock came the sound of the postman. Suddenly my instinct took over and I found myself turning towards the front door barking like mad.

'Nicky din-dins, it's meat and peas,' called the soft voice of my owner. When I had eaten my breakfast I was left alone in the house, unsure of what to do I lay in the living room. I soon got bored of staring into space, I looked around for something to do, a pair of rather fetching slippers caught my eye. Once again my instinct took over and before I knew it I was chewing them up.

When my owners got home they seemed very angry and sent me to the corner in disgrace. I was left alone most of the afternoon until it was time for my walk. At the end of the day I decided that being a dog was not so bad.

Gemma Smith (11)
Bonneygrove Primary School

I Am A Cat

I am a cat, furry and cute,
My eyes are green, they glow in the dark.
I am cat that's black and white,
My tail is long and I hunt in the night.

I pounce on my prey,
It puts up a fight.
It runs really fast, or tries to take flight.
With a nose, or a beak,
It's all yummy to eat.

I am a cat, furry and cute,
My eyes are green, they glow in the dark.
I am a cat that's black and white,
My claws are sharp, my steps are light.

I live in a house,
It's green and red.
My owner she lives there,
I sleep in her bed.

I am a cat, furry and cute,
My eyes are green, they glow in the dark.
I am a cat that's black and white,
My mouth is wide, my teeth shine bright.

When darkness comes,
I creep down the stairs,
Hoping to catch
A mouse unawares.

I am a cat, furry and cute,
My eyes are green, they glow in the dark.
I am a cat, that's black and white,
My senses are sharp, so is my bite.

When luck is out
And there's nothing to eat,
I go to my bowl
For a nice meaty treat.

I am a cat, furry and cute,
My eyes are green, they glow in the dark.
I am a cat, that's black and white,
My tail is long and I hunt in the *night!*

Alexandra Dean (10)
Bonneygrove Primary School

A DAY IN THE LIFE OF A SNAKE!

The fearsome snake
Taunts wildly in the deep jungle,
Endangered with ferocious beasts,
Scattering across the earth's crust.
Moving rapidly, gracefully,
Searching for its prey patiently,
Before opening his razor sharp teeth,
Its jaws wide open!
The courageous snake taking down his prey,
Might raging within him,
He slithers like a curly worm,
A wild night owl,
Like he stares.
Its mosaic, scaly skin,
Stands out in the red-hot sun,
Its eyes are mean,
Clear as glass.
A cautious approach,
By an ugly cockroach,
Too horrible to merrily eat,
So easy to squash are its minute feet.
It lies on it flat,
Until it cries for assistance,
To claim a most helpful resistance,
The cobra's useless prey,
Compared with its might,
To swallow down his bait,
As if he was crunching slate.
He roams the earth from head to tail,
If he hunts he will never fail,
Its venomous sting erupts from his mouth,
He travels rapidly from north to south.

The snake talks with a hissing voice,
Enough to scare a screeching mongoose,
Its body with colours is thin and strong,
The forest where he lives among!

Sam Moss (10)
Bonneygrove Primary School

I AM A HAMSTER

I am a hamster, all grey and white,
I live in a cage full of fun.
The food I may eat is full of energy,
It is yummy for my tummy.
I can play all day in my wheel,
Even climb a bar or two.
My bed is full of shreds
Which I make a hole in to rest.
My face has long whiskers
That I twitch from side to side,
Also a tiny nose all wet and cold.
Cats try and catch me
But I am too fast.
I am awake in the night,
And asleep in the day.
I have Choco Treats, yum, yum, yum.
My claws help me cling on to things,
I climb up cubes to get my exercise.
My owners clean me out and it's all snug.
I had a sister called Squeak
But she died.
We always talked to each other.
We argued who was going in the ball
That rolls round and round.
I was the best at running.
Best of all we had good adventures
And used to get out of the house,
Run up the garden path and
Search! Search! Search!
I can run like a cheetah,
And then drink a litre.

We used to bite the carpet to get out,
And to cut our teeth we know
To gnaw on a sand block.
When my owners have cleaned me out
I mess it up again.
I am just like a human climbing the stairs
To get to the top.

Kelly Belsey (10)
Bonneygrove Primary School

THE MAGIC CLOCK!

One day I was walking through the alley on my way to school when I saw something glisten in the gutter. I bent down to see what the mysterious thing was . . . it was a necklace! I was late for school so I raced my way through the halls. As I got to my class someone shouted, 'Detention.' It was Mrs Lyme staring at me in the face.

All of a sudden the necklace broke and fell to the floor, out popped a grumpy old man with a little white beard. He was a wizard and gave me one wish. I shouted, 'I want to be a clock.'
The wizard said, 'Tick-tock, tick-tock, turn this girl into a magic clock.'

I could not believe it, I was a clock. I knew my five times table. I could go back through time. Oh look, there's Mrs Lyme eating the chocolate I gave her. It is very lonely up here, no one to talk to. Oh it's play time and it my turn to put out the equipment.

'Help, Mrs Lyme help. I am in the clock. Please Mr Wizard help.'

All of a sudden a puff of smoke was in front on me, the scenery had changed, I was back!

Kerry Barnes (10)
Bonneygrove Primary School

LINFORD CHRISTIE

Meet the race I do, waiting eagerly to go,
Stretching and bending whatever I do,
I'm so supple like some dough.
Bang off I go at an incredible pace,
I storm along the ground like a police chase,
Or a tornado flying along.
You can hardly see sweat running down my face,
But am I going to win this exhilarating race?
I pass some more racers,
When I pass them you should see their faces,
The amount of speed I am going,
I could pass you without you knowing.
I was near the finish line,
It was in my sight,
Oh did the leader have a fright.
When I, Linford Christie, past him fast,
I thought I was top class.
I ran through the finish tape,
I puffed and panted and then caught my breath,
'Your record is 5.8,' said the ref.
Well I thought that was another personal best,
Now you know why I am better than the rest!

Rio Tourlamain (11)
Bonneygrove Primary School

A Day In The Life Of A Colonel

I am the colonel
Of the Cateen Army.
Live in the year 40,000
With weird and horrible creatures.

I look just like a human,
Two arms, two legs, two eyes.
Our destiny,
To kill, to destroy, to win.

We do not give any mercy,
All we do is win.
We must defeat
Voldo and the Lachans.

I'm wandering in the forest,
Green leaves, green grass, green suits.
I see dark shapes in the shadows,
And get ready to aim and fire!

We watch, wait and see
Voldo and the Lachans.
All shaded in red,
Their eyes on fire.

We shoot and shoot and shoot,
The Lachans are going down,
All apart from Voldo
Who had killed most of my men.

We run through the forest trees,
Voldo on our tail.
An abandoned tank lay up ahead,
We run there for our life.

Voldo is catching up!
We feel ourselves get thrown.
Nothing had even touched us,
We are falling - falling into the tank.

I get up, my men - dead,
I run to the front and turned it around,
To see Voldo,
Standing - standing all alone.

I aim the machine gun at his chest,
Voldo begs for mercy.
My thumb rests on the button,
And Voldo falls dead on the forest floor.

Victory!
We won,
My home planet cheered,
For Voldo - Voldo had been destroyed.

Now we may rest in peace.

Matthew Chivers (9)
Bonneygrove Primary School

A Day In The Life Of The King Of The Plains

I am the all powerful and great lion,
The ruler and challenger of the Zion.
I fight for my kingdom and pride,
I am then proudly rewarded with a bride.

I roar over the deep dark night,
Which had just been conquered by a brave fight.
Nothing have I done wrong, my lifestyle must be right,
But why then do poachers follow me with all their might?

I lie in peace over the wet plains,
Whilst my fur baths in the rains.
I scan every corner of land in sight,
Desperately in search of something to bite.
For survival is something greatly needed,
Because the greed of man has succeeded.

I spring into action with great hopes,
But with such disastrous conditions I might not cope.
Survival is something I need,
But I also have to help in the battle to save my breed.

Painfully I watch my home being cut away,
With no luck that I shall endure today -
My best have I tried all the time,
To save my forest which is being denied to mine.

Carelessly I drive onto the petrified poachers,
With no fear like a challenging soldier;
Standing no chance I am cut to the grounds,
But like every king I am now worth only pounds.

Giles Safori-Amponsah (11)
Bonneygrove Primary School

THE FRIENDLY SCARE

A tropical fish is what I am,
My glimmering scales are as smooth as sand.
Love to dart and play I do,
And love to nibble on a trout-filled stew.

Sneaking around the sharp corner of glowing coral,
I found a deserted spot.
I noticed a school of pufferfish,
And scared away the lot.
I settled into my new home,
Realising I didn't have to pay any loan!
Life was good, precious and fishy,
It also had a pinch of something delicious.

Instantly there was a blinding flash,
And a distant clang of a tumultuous crash.
Panicking, sweat over-taking me,
I was finding it extremely hard to see.
I darted into a reef of pink coral,
Upset was I, also filled with deep sorrow.

Immediately, I came to my senses,
Realising the sea did *not* have any fences.
That meant what was coming to get me,
Would have no trouble finding the golden key!

A wave of shock, over me it ran,
I felt as if I seriously needed a fan!
Round the corner it lingered quietly,
Suddenly it jumped out and said, 'It's Mr Riley!'
He was only here to kindly give me
A pot of trout-filled stew from his family.

Laura Rockall (11)
Bonneygrove Primary School

A Day In The Life Of Harry Potter

Waking up grumpily as a grizzly bear
Thundering unhappily down to the gigantic food hall
As ravenous as a tiger
It is down with the other hungry Gryffindors
The breakfast is fit for a king
There are sausages, eggs and hash browns
After my breakfast I am refreshed
First lesson quidditch, whoopee.

Strutting over to the Hogwarts forest
The Quidditch ground stands
I pull out my mighty firebolt
One of the fastest brooms around
The mystical box with three balls in is opened
Whoosh! The balls flew gracefully out of the box.

The names are the Bludger, the Quaffle, and the Golden Snitch
The crowd watched in suspense
Also as the Ravenclaw team rise
As one of my team is hit by the Bludger
A ravenclaw races to the Quaffle it moves
There is was the Golden Snitch
I got it
I was hailed with cheers.

My next lesson was the most exciting
Defence against the dark arts
With the great Mad Eye Moody
He skimmed the register
With a watchful eye
Out of its worst for wear desk he got a rat
Half the class shrieked
Hercus, murcus, lurcus Moody thundered
With a sly fox grin
Bizarrely the rat acted like the Hogwarts Express
Seconds later it dropped stone cold dead.

Dinner time arrived
I had beef, Yorkshire puddings
I scoffed it all down
I felt weary
I think about the teachers at Hogwarts
I finally reach the dormitory
Thinking about all the teachers at Hogwarts
Falling into bed
I drown deeper into my dreams.

Gareth Redmond (10)
Bonneygrove Primary School

TURTLE

One morning I had come
From land or sea or sun,
My shell had cracked
And that was that,
So off to sea I swam.

I was taken by the waves
Which washed me in the caves,
I waited for the tide
To take me in my stride,
So off to sea I swam.

In the water I am,
So to a shelter I swam,
There I linger
And watched the finger,
So off to sea I swam.

At last I am three
And with me a glee,
For I have found
My special ground,
So off to sea I swam.

With my shell
And my special girl,
I love to play
Especially in May,
So off to sea I swam.

In a bay I am stranded,
There an aeroplane landed,
To rescue me
They set me free,
So off to sea I swam.

Now I am eight
And ready to mate,
I have a wife
And together we have a fabulous life,
So off to sea I swam.

We swim together
For ever and ever,
We never leave each other's side
Until the morning's tide,
So off to sea I swam.

Now I have kids of my own
And to me they always groan,
But to my wife
They are so very nice,
So off to sea *we* swam.

Jenna Read (10)
Bonneygrove Primary School

LIFE OF A DOG

Hi I'm a dog
And my name is Scruff,
I have a collar
And my fur's in a scruff.

My owner's name is Percy,
He owns a tiny flat,
We like to play together,
On my favourite mat.

One day we went to the park,
In the middle of the town,
It was rainy and wet
Which gave me a frown.

There we played ball
And played with a stick,
I was running from place to place,
Which made me very sick.

I met many dogs there,
Fat, thin, short and tall,
I made many friends there,
Made friends with them all.

We went to the butchers
To get some meat,
I went with my owner,
To buy a new sheet.

Walked home in the pouring rain,
My collar was beginning to rust,
Brown and dirty were my paws,
Instead we caught a bus.

We got home at 5 o'clock,
Just in time for tea,
I was really hungry,
My owner could obviously see.

I walked over to my mat
And there I sat and sunk,
My owner bought my bowl over,
My favourite, Pedigree Chunks.

At 8 o'clock we went to bed,
Percy turned off the light,
Then we fell asleep together,
To everyone, goodnight.

Lauren Carter (10)
Bonneygrove Primary School

THE LIFE OF A DRAGON

Fire burning, tail wagging,
Wings flapping, tongue moving,
Eyes glinting, nail biting dragon,

A soft, gold, pointy tail,
Sharp sparking claws,
All is ready for the dragon of fire,
As he gains up to his prey,

Fire burning, tail wagging,
Wings flapping, tongue moving,
Eyes glinting, nail biting,

The fierce dragon bends down ready to pounce,
Keeping his eyes ready straight to the target,
He counts down from three,

Three, two, one, pounce into the air,
Up into the midnight sky,
Landing straight onto the target, his prey,

Fire burning, tail wagging,
Wings flapping, tongue moving,
Eyes glinting, nail biting,

Who knows what he'll do next?
One eye is sharp,
But the other is blind,

Amazing how he can spot his prey,
And it was a distance away,
I cannot wait for the next time,
It will be even more amazing than the first,

Fire burning, tail wagging,
Wings flapping, tongue moving,
Eyes glinting, nail biting,

The people charm to the dragon, to wake him up,
They carry some food to take to him at the top of the cliff,
Will he fall or will he fly?
I don't know, but I wonder.

Ciham Messouki (11)
Bonneygrove Primary School

THE RABBIT

The colour I am is white as snow,
My eyes are pink and they twinkle like stars,
My coat is so soft, like layers of feathers,
My ears are long, slender, sensitive, my life savers.

I love my home, it is so warm,
Flowers have grown, they are so pretty.
There's lovely grass for me to sit on, it's like a green
Mattress; bouncy and comfy.
My hay is so soft, like a cotton wool ball.
My butterfly friends fly around with such ease,
With beautiful colours floating in the breeze.

My favourite food is carrots and greens,
Twigs and leaves, apples and pears,
I have my eyes on some home grown veg
But I'm sure if I eat it, I will be banished to bed.

The shiny sun is what I like best,
It's a great ball of fire with vigour and zest,
Then it starts raining,
So I hop frantically to the safety of my hutch.

My owner Lauren is so kind,
She loves me and cares so much about me,
She plays with me,
Talks to me,
Sings songs to me
And gently tickles me on my tummy,
When I am with Lauren, I feel so safe and so happy.

But what do you expect from a really cute bunny.

Lora Hammond (10)
Bonneygrove Primary School

FISH

In joy I swam around the tank,
I explored all the past wreckage of a ship,
Particles of drift wood,
Lay on the seabed.

If I were a fish I would swim, swim, swim and explore all
Day, not remember a thing of where I have been.

I have swam around the superb fish tank,
However, I don't know what I done,
Where I have been,
Who I have seen.

A couple of water snails,
Sucks algae off the glass,
Baby toads swim around,
Like flies flying underwater.

I do not know who I am,
My memory is blank,
So this is the end.

Ben Horsman (10)
Bonneygrove Primary School

A Day In The Life Of A Viking

I am a Viking of power,
I am a Viking of the worthy,
I care for no one or nothing,
I live or serve for no one.

I am a mighty Viking,
A leader of a huge army,
I wear fur of savage beasts
And armour as strong as ox's.

We have clashed with the enemy,
The Titans,
Their weaponry is far superior than ours,
We have few archers and our axes
Are not as well made,
But now we fight.

Blood, dead bodies,
Like a horror story come true,
Our spy is back,
His horse is wounded with arrows,
Worst, our spy is headless.

My followers and I are safe,
It was a brutal war,
We have won,
It is time to get to the ship.

Now on my ship after winning a great war,
Success has proven itself.
We come back victorious,
Some were not worthy of us,
As barbaric as it seems, they are gone.

As we sail the seas, a storm occurs,
We may not make it,
But we go to yet another battle,
A battle of the storm,
Huge winds blow us on to the rocks
And to our doom.

I am a Viking of power,
I am a Viking of the worthy,
I care for no one or nothing,
We have crashed.

I am alive,
Yet, my followers are gone forever,
Now I am still on that rock,
A mere skeleton,
Now it will always be remembered as the great . . .

Viking Clash!

Daniel Smith (10)
Bonneygrove Primary School

A DAY IN THE LIFE OF A WHITE TIGER

The white tiger is now extinct, my mate and me are the last white tigers in the world!

Wait, I've just seen my breakfast, jump . . . catch my deer please while I climb up the tree.

Hey don't eat any, pass a half here.

I live in India, OK leopards wait in the trees. We don't but I saw one and that's why I'm doing the same.

'Let's go to a lake and get a drink.'

Aaahh that was a nice drink, wasn't it? I'm going to have a nap, OK. Yawn. What a lovely nap. I'm going to get some lunch, look there's a buffalo, lovely and tender, isn't it? I'm going for a walk, coming?

Loren Clark (9)
Brushwood Junior School

A DAY IN THE LIFE OF A WOLF

I like being a wolf, even though I don't like to look at blood. It's freezing out here. Mmmm, grub, a jackal. I missed! I'm going to try again, got you, yes little pip squeak, mmmm tasty! A penguin even better, missed oh no I'm skidding across the ice. Straight into . . . ffffrrreeezzziiinnnggg . . . water. Yes back on land, what's that fluffy white thing? I'm very close. Sheesh kebabs, what a close shave. Wow what a fast thing it is. I think it's a polar bear, it is, it is!

I like it in the North Pole. Here's my pack now, we will have revenge on the polar bear, yes revenge at last. Now feast mmmmm! Lovely feast. I am going into my den where the cubs are playing. Before I got there, a penguin slid down so I jumped on top of the penguin. Wow what a catch. Now how will I tell the cubs about the story of my life.

Daniel Lathwell (9)
Brushwood Junior School

A DAY IN THE LIFE OF A TUDOR SAILOR

Dear Dominic,

We're still on HMS Hedwick, we've nearly reached our lost ocean and then we will have sailed the Seven Seas, can you believe it?

I've got some bad news though, my best mate Matthew dramatically died a few weeks ago, while he was climbing the rigging (there was a broken rope) it is so horrible being a sailor you can die any minute.

The food is grim but we stay cheerful getting drunk on our rations of brandy, ale and rum.

About 5 weeks ago we were attacked by native people and we lost 20 men.

We captured a very powerful ship a week ago and they had the most popular and amazing weapons. Now we've got them, ha!

A few weeks later, while we were in the Pacific we stumbled across a Spanish ship. They weren't expecting an English ship to be there as well so a blast from our new weapons and they were ours! Drake was pleased because they had a good pilot, who will now help us navigate.

Still more bad news! Drake died in Spain, we were very devastated because he was our best captain but he's still with us as a spirit making sure we get home safely.

Hope you and your family are well?

The Crew Member - Jack Rivans

Jack Rivans (10)
Brushwood Junior School

A Day In The Life Of A Tudor Sailor

HMS Pelican
Indian Ocean
Southern Hemisphere

23rd May 1501

Dear Queen Elizabeth,

I am writing to tell you how our voyage is going. We are on a ship called the Pelican and we are sailing over the equator. We have been sailing for three months now and the storms have been quite bad.

We have found new countries and we have put them on our maps. We started off at Plymouth with 349 men and we have now lost 49 of them. Our diet has been mixed, eating food like salted beef, seals, dried pork, penguins and special biscuits and we have been drinking just beer and water. We have been sailing round the world for three years now and we are absolutely exhausted.

We have found some treasure on the Spanish and Portuguese ships. Our ship was damaged but we found some bits and pieces to fix it with. Some men were injured a lot, they had been bandaged by the surgeon, but some sailors survived.

We have found some treasure on the Spanish and Portuguese ships. Our ship was damaged but we found some bits and pieces to fix it with. Some men were injured a lot, they have had to be bandaged by the surgeon, some of them survived.

My journey has been wonderful,

Yours faithfully
Captain Edward Cooper

Rahena Hoque (10)
Brushwood Junior School

A DAY IN THE LIFE OF CHRISTOPHER GILBERT

I'm Christopher Gilbert, I'm a dad to my twin children Sophie and Haydn and a husband to my wife Tracey. I have a brother Paul and a sister, Angie. I am the boss of the taxi firm Gilbert's of Chesham.

Today I have the day off work, the children are at school and Tracey is working. She's just phoned me and she's asked me to do the housework, so I'm standing here now with the hoover next to me. Wahey and it's off. Where's it gone now? Bang!

All of a sudden the hoover bag has split and the dirt and dust when all over me and the furniture. 'What's Tracey going to say?' I said. After I had washed and changed, I put the dirty washing in the machine and off it whirled. I turned round and I saw smoke. I looked at the machine. It had exploded! When I had mopped up, I started cleaning the TV, then the world changed.

I saw spotlights and cameras and just then I wasn't watching TV, I was in it. A person behind me with a big camera told me it was my turn on the stage. I asked him what programme we were doing and he said Neighbours from Hell. He told me I was the neighbour from hell which meant I was a noisy neighbour and I wasn't noisy but deep down, I knew I wasn't telling the truth in the programme. I was frightened because everybody was looking at me and they wanted to gang up on me.

As they were walking towards me, I could feel a shiver down my spine, the next thing I knew I was out of the TV.

I was sitting on the sofa when Tracey came in saying 'What's this mess!' I said, 'Sorry I had a bit of an accident.' I cleaned up with Tracey and I never will tell her or my children about being on TV. It's a secret.

Sophie Gilbert (9)
Brushwood Junior School

A Day In The Life Of A Dog

Hello my name is Scamp the dog, now this story is about me when I ran away. Even me, a cool dog, was scared.

Once when I was a pup and I wasn't allowed out, I was playing with the 3 year old baby. His name was Oliver. I noticed the window was open. I jumped through the window, I heard a few barks and shouts. I ran and jumped the wall, they were junkyard dogs, so I ran away with them.

When I got to the junkyard, Dodger, the leader dog examined me, 'So what's your name?' said Dodger.

'Name's Scamp.'
'Well Scamp want to join us?'
'Yeah sure.'
'Well you will have to do some tests.'

So they did some tests on me, my first test was to steal a chicken leg off a boat, but just as I was about to leave the boat, it went, worst of all it was the last boat to America. 4 hours later we were there. I wasn't going to spend 5 minutes on this island. I jumped out to sea and swam back home.

When I got about half way home, sharks surrounded me, then crash! Bang! It was a mermaid. She got me in her arms and said 'Don't worry little pup, I'll carry you home.' 4 hours later, I woke up on my front door, I ran in the door to my bed and got my bone to chew.

Now I am grown up but that happened 9 years ago.

Heather Lansdell (9)
Brushwood Junior School

A DAY IN THE LIFE OF A HORSE

Hello my name's Kerry and I'm a horse.

I've just woken up from a deep sleep. Mrs Penny should be here soon to take me into the field.

Here she is now. 'Come on old boy,' said Mrs Penny.

Mrs Penny is an old lady, she has a bad eye because of all the dust in the stables. It gathered up in her left eye, she says she can't understand how we horses live with it.

'Now you be good, Sue's going to ride you and I don't want you caked in mud Kerry! I want you to be on your best behaviour!'

Sue rode me into the woods, I stopped, there was a fox, it jumped up at me, my shoulder was bleeding.

I bucked and bolted. Sue fell and rolled down into a ditch, her face was covered in mud.

The fox leaped up onto my back, his teeth sank deep into my flesh, there was blood everywhere.

Just when I was about to give up, I saw some people walking by, I whinnied, they stopped and ran over, the fox had gone. They took hankies from their bags and rubbed my shoulder with them. I limped over to Sue, they gasped, the two men climbed down to her, lifted her out and put her in the recovery position while the two ladies ran to a phone box and rang 999 for an ambulance.

The ambulance came and a lady got out with three men. Two men took care of Sue while the lady and a man looked at my cut and walked me into a horse box.

When we were all safely back at the stables, Mrs Penny sent Sue up to bed with a mug of hot chocolate. I went to bed with a bandage around my leg, mmmmmm fresh hay, ohhh ahhh eeeh soft, straw. Well goodnight all. Ohhh, ahhh, eeehh, zzzzz.

Helen Shepherd (9)
Brushwood Junior School

A Day In The Life Of My Dog

Hello, I am Jasper, James MacLeod is my pet. He thinks I'm his pet, but that's just plain nonsense.

Oh no, walkies! Anything but walkies, why me? When I was a puppy, it was fine because it was only once round the block, now it's about fifty times round the block, I hate it.

Mum is coming with the collar, it will be on my neck any minute. Just a sec! It's the BT phone thing, here we go, this is it. The door's open and I'm out!

Huh, I just bumped into a man with green trousers and a T-shirt with a red line through a dog on it. Run for it! He's getting into a van. I'm past the corner now, I am flying by, here they come but they don't stand a chance against my speed and agility.

I have now gone round the block ten times, I think they have lost me. I have gone into my home just in case. Ah here is mum, let's see what she has to say 'Walkies Jasper,' oh no!

James Macleod (9)
Brushwood Junior School

A Day In The Life Of Paul Gasgoine

Hi I'm Paul Gasgoine, I am 33 years old and I live in Gateshead. I used to play for Spurs but now I play for Everton. I made my debut in the premiership at the age of 18 and was playing for Newcastle. Football is my favourite hobby.

I have to keep myself healthy by eating things like vegetables and pasta, and I need to drink water or milk, I normally have pasta, vegetables, turkey, and milk to drink. For my breakfast I have a cup of tea or coffee and cereal with no sugar in either. For lunch I have a sandwich and crisps.

At about 12.00pm I set off to get to the training ground. I train at my home ground Goodison Park. Just before the match, I stretch and I run up and down the field a couple of times.

At 3.00pm, the ref blows his whistle for the start of Everton vs. Bradford. The match was under way, 15 minutes had gone and it was 1-0 to Bradford already. Just before half-time, Duncan Ferguson equalised. In the second half, Everton struck again, this time Nicolas Alexander. After that it just went Everton's way, the final score, 2-1 to Everton.

I was injured early in the second half and I had to be taken off. I was very sad because I had been out with injury most of the season.

At the end of my day, I set off home for pasta and milk or if I'm lucky a cup of tea. I rest my injured leg while watching TV then I go safely to bed after all the excitement.

Neil Padbury (9)
Brushwood Junior School

A DAY IN THE LIFE OF MY SISTER

Hello, I'm Hannah. I've got a brother called James. I live in Chesham, Bucks. I am four years old and I've got blonde hair. I go to nursery every weekday unless it's the holiday.

I am on my camping holiday in the Isle Of Wight, I'm going to an adventure park called Black Gang Chine.

'Hannah, time to get in the car,' called Mum. We all climbed in and Dad drove off. The adventure park wasn't that far away from the camp site.

When we got there we decided to go on a water slide. The ride had a few big bumps in it and it wasn't very long. We had to wait in a long queue. When we were in the queue I felt a bit scared. When I saw all the other people that were going down the ride screaming I felt really frightened. But when we got to the top of the ride I was really, really frightened but I still wanted to go on it. To go down the ride you had to go in a dinghy. I went in a dinghy with my dad. When the ride started we shot down it at a terrific speed. I got to the bottom and I was crying. I got back to Mum and I said, 'I want to go on it again,' but we didn't have enough time to do that.

We went on lots of other fun rides like a maze and a dinosaur park. In the dinosaur park there were really tall dinosaurs that made noises. When we went in there I started to think the dinosaurs were real and they would eat me, but then I realised they weren't real, they were only pretend. After we'd been in the dinosaur park we went to the big maze with high hedges. I thought I'd like to go and explore it by myself, like my brother James. So I went in, I weaved in and out of the hedges. I kept coming to dead ends. Eventually I managed to get out the exit then I rushed back in the exit and James had to come and find me and help me get out. But I got out before James. James got stuck, he kept trying and then he got out.

After all the fun at Black Gang Chine we went back to the camp site. Back at the camp site it was very windy but luckily our tent was still standing. We all had dinner, I was sitting at my high chair, I fell asleep in it. Mum got me out from my high chair and put my pyjamas on me, then she put me in my sleeping bag and said good night.

James Warren (9)
Brushwood Junior School

A DAY IN THE LIFE OF A HOUSE MOUSE

Hi, I'm Harvey the house mouse and I hate being a mouse! I'm so small. Nothing in the house is smaller than me, not even the other mice! I wish I was a big strong rat. I live in a big fancy house with five sets of big ridges going up (humans call them stairs). I live at the top of the first set of ridges in a little hole.

'I'm going for a walk,' I said to Dad.
'Okay,' he said.

I ran out of the hole and under a big soft thing people sit on. I sat there and watched people clump by. When no one was around I raced out across the floor.

'Aaaaeeeeek!' screamed a person! Bother they've spotted me, I raced under the big soft thing and hid there.
'It's a rat, we'll phone the council,' said a person's voice.

When it was all clear I crept out from under the soft thing and headed back to the hole. 'Thump' a net fell down on me. I tried to get it off me but it was too heavy, I was trapped. A man took me in a net to a van and dropped me in a cage. I looked around, there where a lot of mice in the cage too and a lot of sawdust on the floor. Then something leapt out of a pile of sawdust, a rat! I dodged, but its claws ripped my side. I dodged into a pile of sawdust. I heard the rat getting closer to the pile of sawdust I was hiding in. I then jumped out and I sank my teeth into the rat's throat, it fell down dead. I had killed a rat! No mouse had ever done that! Right, now to escape. I started gnawing a the cage door but it was metal. I'd better try to break it down. 'Bash, crash, smash!' Yes, I've broken down the door. I ran out and into the cab then I jumped out of a window. 'Thump' I landed on something that humans call the pavement. I ran along at top speed, I ran all day until I came to a large building, I ran inside.

'Scrreea,' screamed a rat as it leapt out on me. I jumped aside and bit its throat, and once again I had killed a rat.

I ran up the ridges and when I saw the mouse hole I realised I was home. I tore towards the mouse hole, but stopped. There was a wooden gate at the mouse hole entrance. I cautiously approached the gate.

'Dad,' I called, 'Dad.'
'Is that you Harvey?' Dad called,
'Dad, open the gate,' I said.
With a slight clank the gate opened. Dad was in there with all the other mice, the hole had been made a lot bigger.
'Dad, why are all the mice here and why was there a rat?' I asked.
'So,' said Dad, 'you saw a rat.'
'No,' I said, 'I killed it.'
A sudden silence fell in the room.
'You killed a rat?' exclaimed Dad.
'Yes,' I said.
It didn't take long to explain while I had been away rats had taken over.
'Well,' I said, 'we've got to fight back!' and that's what we did. We attacked the rat stronghold in the cellar and destroyed it. We sent those rats running!

During the attack I killed the great rat. We all now live as we did before - happily.

Stefan Ellender (8)
Brushwood Junior School

A DAY IN THE LIFE OF MY SISTER MOLLY

Hello my name is Molly Neary. I live in a normal street and I live in a plain house. My house is small but my room is nice. I have to share it with my sister Chloe. We have to share most of our things including our wardrobe, Chloe takes up all the space with her clothes, well not all the space.

Chloe and me always argue, it's always her fault but I get blamed, it's horrible when I get blamed, but what I am about to tell you is better. I get congratulated.

Today we're going to a London Theatre. Chloe says we have to go to some shops first but we don't really have to. An hour later, we are here at last, we've got good seats, this is beautiful. An hour later, I'm thirsty. I'm going to ask for a drink, mum says I can go if Chloe goes with me. 'OK she can.' 2 minutes later, I smell fire, Chloe says 'Let's go and see,' so we do! Yes it is fire, we both shouted fire! Fire!

Chloe runs to mum and mum runs to the manger, he puts the fire alarm on and phones the fire brigade.

3 minutes later, the manager said 'Well done,' to Chloe and me. 'You've saved thousands of lives' and he gave me and Chloe a bag full of 50 pound notes. We are rich!

5 minutes later, guess what? We have brought a mansion and we only got the money 5 minutes ago, life is beautiful but there's one thing missing, me and Chloe haven't argued, I think I will go and pick an argument with her just this once.

He, he, hi, hi, he, he.

Chloe Neary (9)
Brushwood Junior School

A Day In The Life Of A Rabbit

I hate being a rabbit, having to eat cabbage and carrots and being stuck in this hutch. Why can't I live in that big hutch at the top of the garden? It's better than flies nipping off you every day. At least my owners look after me. But I hate the way they stroke me!

The good thing about my owners is they give me a treat every Sunday. They give me an oat biscuit. Wahoo! They are lifting me up again. Bump. Why don't they let me in the house?

Hmm, if I can get through these bars I can escape. Well, I'll start trying. Here it goes, urrh, I'm through. It's nice to be free. I had better get going, the cat's due any second.
'Bongie, Bongie!' So this is what it looks like next door.

So this is a road. There are big black monsters trying kill me and stones flicking up behind. How am I going to get across? I'll have to wait till there are no giant lawnmowers. Time to cross the road. Just another half way, uhoh. Fancy being caught on a lawnmower.

Can I hear footsteps? It's human help. I'm being lifted up I can feel the soft hair like mine and warm fur-like hair of a human. This feels nicer than my owners. Where's she taking me. Woo, there's loads of rabbits and they're all inside. Perhaps it will be better living with other rabbits.

Jake Dumbarton (9)
Brushwood Junior School

A DAY IN THE LIFE OF TRACEY GILBERT

I am Tracey, a wife and mum to Christopher and my twins Haydn and Sophie. I work seven hours a day. I work as a part-time hairdresser and a partner in a taxi firm.

I called Haydn and Sophie for school and started driving up the hill. I dropped off the children and started driving. As I was driving down the road the car started getting slower then 'Bang!' The engine started smoking. It wasn't really my car, it was Christopher's. I got out my mobile phone and phoned Chris to tell him the bad news. After I had phoned Chris the car set fire! After the firemen had been I started walking home.

After I had my lunch, I went to the back garden to see how the builders were doing. Oh no, I haven't told you, I'm having an extension on the house! The builders asked if they could go.
I replied, 'Yes, you can go now.'

I walked outside with my mobile phone in my pocket, looking up I took a step out and 'Bang!' With cement up my nose I had fallen down the hole! After pulling myself out I went to the bathroom to get washed and dry. First I was going to wash my face so I walked up to the sink and I was just about to put the plug in the plughole when I saw some soap near the plughole so I poked my finger down the plughole a little and the soap went down the hole as normal. I pulled out my finger but it didn't come out! Pulling out my mobile phone with one hand I phoned Chris. I tugged on my finger but it still wouldn't come out! In the end Chris phoned the fire brigade.

When the fire brigade came they had to go back to the burned car. After half an hour the whole brigade were trying to pull out my finger. In the end the fire brigade got out the big metal cutters. When the brigade had finished and gone my finger felt horrible.

The children skidded in from school shouting they wanted to go on a bike ride. I thought that's all I need. So I walked up the hill and 'Bang! Oh no! That's all I need.'

Haydn Gilbert (9)
Brushwood Junior School

DAY IN THE LIFE OF HARRY POTTER

Hi, I'm Harry. I love being a wizard. I have the best friends in all of Hogwarts, Hermione and Ron. Right now I am sitting up in my bed in the Gryffinder dormitory. My worst lesson is with Snape - potions! The one thing I would like to know is what is it like to be a muggle? At least you wouldn't have to do potions with Snape and you wouldn't have to know Draco Malfoy. Anyway, gotta go, time for potions.

I'm sitting in potions now, ready for Snape to come in.
'Good morning Snape,' the rest of the class and I said together.
Then Snape said, 'We are going to turn a frog into a snake,' in such a cold tone, 'right, get this and that and done.'
'Sorry, I talk while I work.' Suddenly Ron turned to look at me. I looked round and part of him had turned into a lizard . . .
'Oh brother!'

'It's time for lunch now, oh no, what about Ron, he's a lizard.' When we got in there people started to whisper about what they thought was my lizard. Just then Professor Dumbledore came up to me and asked if I could go and have a talk.
Half an hour later, I came out, 'He just told me that Ron's spell went a bit wrong and we were going to turn him back.'

After lunch Hermione and I went into the library and there we found the right spell, we said the spell and there in front of us was . . . Ron! Then suddenly we found ourselves in, in somewhere, we looked at the sign it read 'Logsreed', we're in Logsreed. We had to look to see if we could find a spell to take us back. Well we went into about five shops and bought some things with some money we found. After that we did find the spell to take us back (after Hermione bought around five books). When at last we did get back it was 10 o'clock so we crept back to bed!

I would love to have a day like that - wouldn't you?

Georgia Parry-Jones (9)
Brushwood Junior School

A Day In The Life Of Neil Armstrong

One day I was so excited. I tripped down the stairs.

'Help!' I shouted, rolling backwards. I hit the wall.
At the spaceship I was shouting, 'Wait for me,' but it was a test run.
They said, 'Come, have a cup of coffee.'
I said, 'Yes please.'

I burnt my tongue. I forgot to stir it and put milk in it. Now I am getting in my spaceship. I tripped again. I finally read the side, it said Apollo 11. The people who came with me were Buzz Aldrin, he was the second on the moon after me and Michael Collins, he was driving the command module - the part that went down to the moon.

At home a crowd of people cheered us back. 'Hooray, hip hip hooray, hip hip hooray.'

Keith Francis (9)
Brushwood Junior School

A Day In The Life Of My Dad

One Thursday morning my dad got up as usual and went downstairs to get a drink before going to work. My dad's a lorry driver and every morning he gets in his lorry, he starts the engine and drives off.

He was on his way to Aylesbury. He was working near a go-karting place. When he got there he said to himself, 'I feel tired, I think I might go go-karting for an hour'.

He parked his lorry and went to get some overalls on. He got in the go-kart and went around the track. On his sixth lap he crashed into the barrier.

The man came and put him back on the track. He went around the bend and skidded, he made a big skid mark. On the twelfth lap he crashed again and he blew up the go-kart engine so he went back to his lorry. When he was on his way home he got a flat tyre so he went to his yard in Watford to get his tyre changed. When he had his tyre done he went home. On the way home on the by-pass his engine blew up so he got his mobile phone out but it had no service on it and it had just started to rain, so he got his jacket on and tried to find a phone. He found a phone so he phoned the AA and they came out to him with a pick-up truck. So they took my dad home and they took the lorry to be fixed.

Two weeks later he went to pick up his lorry and went back to work.

Scott Atkins (9)
Brushwood Junior School

A DAY IN THE LIFE OF A TUDOR SEAMAN

The Warrior
In The Atlantic Ocean

Dearest Mother and Father

I feel lonely, sick, tired, sad and bored. The ship is very big and its name is Warrior.

It has lasted two hurricanes and dangerous battles against the pirates. All I can see is water and sky and smell the sea, air and wind. Lots of people have died today. I am one of the few who made it. I have just been sent up the rigging to see why we're going in circles. We were in a whirlpool so we went in a life boat and escaped.

Your loving son Ishaq

Ishaq Munir (10)
Brushwood Junior School

A DAY IN THE LIFE OF A TUDOR SEAMAN

The Endeavour
Somewhere in The Atlantic Ocean
Oct 15th 1579

Dearest Father

The weather is nice and sunny here in the dock. I am nearly dehydrating but it is better than the rain. I think there are diseases on board but I'm not too sure. I have already been sea sick two times but I feel alright now.

I have just left and I seem to be getting on with other cabin boys. I have met one called Charles, he's a nice boy. The ship is called The Endeavour.

The food is quite nice compared to what we have. When I eat, I always sit next to my friend Charles. My favourite food is crackers and a little bit of butter.

I have a job, the job is to clean the guns and the deck and to keep them shiny. Charles has to stand in the crow's nest and look out for enemy ships.

I am missing my friends back home but I have made new ones. I feel this is going to be a very good exploring trip. I sleep on a soft mattress and put a soft sheet over me to keep me warm.

We haven't had many attacks from other ships, just two and we didn't even get hit and I got on their ship and stole their food. We have just landed on an island and called it America.

I wrote two letters back last time, you must not have got them. There must have been a problem in the post office or something. Well I hope you get this letter and read it by the time I'm back. Well I got to go now. Please reply.

Sincerely yours

From your loving son Stewart.

Stewart King (10)
Brushwood Junior School

A Day In The Life Of A Tudor Seaman

The Warrior
Atlantic Ocean
October 1579

Dearest Mother,

I miss you a lot. I am very afraid of diseases and food poisoning. It is my first day out on the ship. We have robbed one ship and got 11 bars of silver and two chests of gold. I am very afraid of scurvy and typhoid. I don't know if I have bite rat disease. We have had no storms yet. The food is disgusting and the biscuit is awful and the meat is salted and rotten. The ship I am on is a galleon with eight canoes in very good condition. The ship is called the Warrior. I don't want bite rat disease. If I do get it, I don't know what I would do without you Mother.

I don't think we will see more natives in the meantime. There is no dangers yet but we had some big waves but that is all. We had a traitor and he's dead now. I want to get a new captain because the one we have shot someone and I want to go home. I want to go home because the captain made me climb the rigging to fix the ropes in windy weather. And afterwards I was told to watch the hourglass. After that he told me to wash the very dirty food pots.

Later I made friends with the other cabin boys. At the time they were cleaning the guns. I found their names out, the first boy is called Johney and the second is called John. Their was another cabin boy but he got shot because he did not work hard. Later John got threatened by the captain. I want to get off this ship. The crew are just like the captain. Afterwards one of the crew tried to escape by jumping overboard but some sharks killed him.

From your loving son Kyle.

Kyle Brunyee (9)
Brushwood Junior School

A DAY IN THE LIFE OF A TUDOR SEAMAN

The Endeavour
Somewhere In The Atlantic
October 15th 1579

Dearest Mother

The weather hasn't been the best I've ever seen in my life. It is windy which is making the boat go quicker which means I should see you sooner.

The chances of living are very slim for me. I just can't keep on doing all their work, it is making me feel sick and too tired. My rules are so hard to conduct, but they are for my safety. The cabin boys that help me work even harder than I do. Plus my work is the hardest job I have ever done for a very, long time.

Life onboard isn't too frustrating for me. I like sleeping on deck but it's breezy for me and my friends. They have explored before me which does disappoint me a bit because they are used to it. My job is cleaning guns for Sir Francis Drake. He is the best captain in the whole wide world. I hope you see me again! I'm too scared of the other ships. The food is all maggoty, it's making me retch. For lunch I had some manky biscuits and some ale to go with it.

Love from your most loved son William.

William Stemman (10)
Brushwood Junior School

A Day In The Life Of A Tudor Seaman

The Elizabeth
America
Dec 4th 1579

Dearest Mother

We have just arrived off the south coast of America. We've just finished scrubbing the deck. We were going to see the native Americans and to stock up on the food and water supplies.

We have been getting worried a bit on the ship because we don't know how long we are going to be out on the ship and how long we are going to live for and whether we are going to get diseases like scurvy and typhoid.

The weather is very stormy here especially when it is splashing the deck and it makes it very hard to scrub the deck when it's stormy because the boat rocks and makes me feel sick.

It's very hard work scrubbing the deck, climbing the rigging, scrubbing the filthy dishes and pans, cleaning the gun and the best job so far on the ship is watching the hourglass.

Abigail Rawlins (10)
Brushwood Junior School

A DAY IN THE LIFE OF A TUDOR SEAMAN

The Endeavour
Somewhere In The Atlantic Ocean
October 15th 1579

Dearest Mother

I am at the port getting ready to set sail. The ship's called Endeavour. Her sail is very grand and big, it has a lion on it.

Life on board a sailing ship is very hard. All the rest of the crew have been on a ship before. The captain's name is Drake. He is a very fine man, he is polite and understands what we feel like to leave our homes.

One of my worst jobs is to watch the half an hour clock. it is so boring and hard.

I have two friends Jim and Jake who have been telling me the worst danger is scurvy.

Oh no! The rain is coming. Sounds like a bad storm.

There's the captain calling for me to help the rest. The lightning has struck the sail and the sail has fallen on Bob. Bob was very nice and fun. I went down, down below deck to get the sail maker. Jim had to bring the dead body down below deck. At first I wanted to go but I had to help fix the sail.

Afterwards we had dinner, it was five biscuits and some salted meat.

Thank you Mum for the fruit cake.

From your loving son Tom.

Naomi Williams (10)
Brushwood Junior School

A Day In The Life Of A Tudor Seaman

The Elizabeth
Somewhere in the Atlantic Ocean
Oct 15th 1579

Dearest Mother and Father

I am about to set off for about thirty weeks. I am scared of storms, we might meet pirates and they might kill us. We eat dry biscuits. I climb the rigging to the crow's nest, then I watch the hourglass but later I clean the filthy food pots. I wash the deck with a scrubbing brush. We are scared of shipwrecks. I miss you.

From your loving son Daniel.

Danielle Sheppard (10)
Brushwood Junior School

A Day In The Life Of A Tudor Seaman

The Warrior
Somewhere in the Atlantic Ocean
Oct 15th 1580

Dearest Mother

The storms have been fierce. I have caught scurvy and diarrhoea. We have bad water. It has been cramped conditions. I wish you were the cook, the food is rotten.

The ship is called the Warrior. We have seen a lot of dolphins. Don't worry about me, hopefully we won't get shipwrecked. I've made some friends. We have dodged some coral reefs. It was really hard to leave you.

There are over sixty people on the ship. The captains are called Ash, Wesley and Charlie. The cook keeps on sneezing in the food. The work is hard. I have to keep on climbing up the rigging to the crow's nest, wash the deck with a scrubbing brush, clean the filthy food pots, clean the guns and watch the hourglass. The food is kept in barrels and the maggots crawl in.

From your loving son Jack.

Jack Read (10)
Brushwood Junior School

A Day In The Life Of Samina

My auntie Samina woke up to go to the library. She got dressed and went, she was twenty-two years old.

When she arrived at the library she met her friends. Their names were Chan who was twenty-five and Amara who was twenty-three. Amara told Samina that they had done their exam revision. The exam was on Saturday. Samina said if they would like to come over to her place. It was Friday today and the exam was tomorrow but Samina said she would do her revision later. After, Samina completely forgot about the exam revision and instead of staying home and revising they all went to a science museum party. Chan drove the car, Samina read the map and Amara stared out the window and stuffed her mouth with sandwiches. When they arrived they got out and opened the big rusted door. It was as if they were entering a haunted house, the lights gloomily turned on but still they were not very clear. Samina, Chan and Amara were standing on something that was moving a little, on a big screen it said, *'Please be seated'* and the thing they were sitting on went faster and faster by the minute, it was as fast as a cat chasing a mouse. Then Samina realised what it was, it was a . . . it was a . . . roller coaster . . . ahhh!

When they got off Amara and Chan couldn't stop talking about it. After they had something to eat, still in the gloomy dark, they had kebabs and pitta bread with curry. Next they went to read a book about science, there was an arrow on another screen saying 'chair boat' Samina and her two friends quietly read a book and suddenly Samina heard a slushy sound of water. Samina saw it coming at them. It splashed over them, they got drenched, they couldn't believe how much fun they were having. The next ride was a ghost train, there's nothing really to explain about that. It's just a ride that you see in a normal fun fair, but there were still far more rides to go on, but suddenly Samina remembered about her exam She kept saying last ride, last ride but then it was time to go because the museum was closing down. When they went back through the rusted door, their car had gone!

The three friends sat on the pavement staring at the cars passing by. Then Samina had a really bad idea, she was thinking like a snail, the idea was for them to stand in the middle of the road and shout 'give us a lift', they tried it, but the cars kept on beeping and Amara nearly got run over, so that didn't work. Amara said 'Let's creep on to the . . . naa! Or let's . . . naa!' Now it was 10 o'clock they stayed there for at least two hours, but then they did find the car, it was halfway down a road called Alexander Hill, it looked as though it had been rolling down.

Home at last, Samina stayed up all night practising for her exam. Today was the exam. Samina's final mark was 72% Chan's final mark was 63% and Amara's final mark was 59%.

Rizwana Ahmed (11)
Brushwood Junior School

A DAY IN THE LIFE OF A TUDOR SEAMAN

Dolphin
Somewhere in The Atlantic Ocean
Oct 15th 1579

Dearest Mother

I'm really scared, I spoke to my friends about the conditions, they said our water is going to turn bad and we will have to have rotten food. A seaman said we might have storms and shipwrecks. Another one said we might get scurvy and die. The thing I am glad about is that we might find treasure. The ship's name is Dolphin and is very big.

We have set sail and I feel sea sick. I don't like being responsible for keeping the ship clean. You have to wash nearly everything. At the end of the day I felt so tired I could sleep for a week. When it was supper time they gave me biscuits.

Later as night fell a storm came, it was a big one. The waves crashed against the side of the ship, I thought we were going to get shipwrecked but we didn't.

After the storm we all had something to eat and drink. My drink was yellow and my biscuit was green. I felt sick afterwards, I slowly walked back to my bed and sat down and fell asleep. I wish I could come back home soon.

By your loving son George.

Catherine Collins (10)
Brushwood Junior School

A Story In The Life Of Thierry Henry

I'm Thierry Henry, I have an important day of football, Arsenal have got through to the finals of the FA Cup. We are going to play in the Millennium Stadium, Cardiff. I hope we win against Liverpool. I know this will be a hard game. I think this is our starting line-up. David Seaman in goal, Dixon at right-back, A Cole at left-back, right centre-back will be Adams, also Martin Keown left centre-back, midfield I think we will have Parlour, Vieira, Grimandi and Pires and up front should be me (Henry) and Wiltord.

Me and Wiltord have a great partnership, I always say two players for the same country make a great partnership, just like me and Wiltord. I just would like another lift of a cup. I got to Highbury and Lee Dixon's car was there. I walked into the stadium and found Lee. We both went out, our cars were gone. We phoned the police and they said 'You parked on a double yellow line.' Our car was waiting at the dump, you have to pick them up by Friday, it is now Sunday. We stood worried thinking what to do . . .

Luke Hayes (10)
Brushwood Junior School

A Day In The Life Of A Tudor Sailor

HMS The Skeleton
Black Sea
23rd may 1501

Dear Father

I am on a boat called The Skeleton, I am the captain. I went out in a storm. On the boat huge waves nearly threw me over board. You know that we have been sailing for four months and in all that time we have been on battles with other captains. Most of my crew have died by fighting.

Our food on board is salted meat, beef and biscuits. We drink beer, ale, wine and fresh water. I am really glad I have got weapons to kill the seagulls because they keep taking my food.

I've got a lot of crew on board with me, I've got men who clean the boat. I have got men who cook the yummy food and two men who are at the look out point. All these men work very hard.

I hope to see you soon,
Captain Spike.

Nicola Smith (10)
Brushwood Junior School

A Day In The Life Of A Tudor Sailor

HMS Eagle
Somewhere in the Indian Ocean
23rd May 1503

Dear Elizabeth

A lot has happened since I last wrote to you. We all have changed our socks every day and we are still keeping to our normal diet, ship's biscuits, seal, penguin and sauerkraut.

We have been attacked by the native Indians and in that battle we lost four of our shipmates.

We have raided a Spanish ship and got lots of gold and silver and we treated ourselves to the Spanish boat.

About a week ago we got attacked again by the Indians, we slaughtered them but I got struck by an arrow below my right eye. We are still travelling strong but we did have one problem. One of our crew told someone in Spain that you sent us so he chose to die by the axe. We all can't wait to get back to England and show you what we have got.

We are just about to sail across the sea and can't wait to get back.

I have to go now.

Yours sincerely
Captain Matt and the crew.

Matthew Ball (9)
Brushwood Junior School

A Day In The Life Of A Tudor Sailor

HMS Seagull
Caribbean
19th March 1515

Dear Queen Elizabeth

Now we're in the Caribbean, it smells a lot because of rubbish, we're all very hot and tired. We're searching for land.

'Land!' The lookout has just shouted! I must go and observe, I shall describe it to you as soon as I can.

There are some beautiful trees, I know they're palm trees. We've been through a lot. Like getting stuck on a reef and nearly sinking. We were caught in a storm when we nearly got blown away with mountainous waves. We were attacked by the native Indians as well. We have lost quite a few men, in all twenty-five out of fifty aboard the Seagull mostly because of the ropes breaking.

We are surrounded by the unusual sound of seagulls, wind on sails, shouts, cries, waves, cranking, creaking wood, guns and dolphins splashing. We really like the food you gave us. The salted meat, Spanish beef, biscuits and the ale, wine, brandy, rum and beer. Thanks for the gun, we shot some penguins and seals. They are really yummy and really filling.

I and my shipmates are very thankful for all the food and things you gave us. We have still got five months sailing to do till we go back but we may have many more dangers ahead of us.

We've sailed the six seas but we have still got one sea to go - the Indian Ocean. So God please make no danger too rough.

I'll write again,
Captain Ziggy.

Zoe Gates (10)
Brushwood Junior School

A Day In The Life Of A Tudor Sailor

HMS Newman
Australia
23rd May 1538

Dear Angelica,

It's great being a captain. You get to name lands. I'm missing you but we'll be home in about 2 years. 'Happy Birthday.'

It has been a bit windy and we changed boats the other day to one called 'The Newman'. Sorry my writing's so bad, the lamp keeps swaying. We changed boats because in the storm everything on our old boat broke so we fought some pirates and won, so now we've got a strong boat and fresh supplies.

The food's not bad, at the moment, I can smell tuna stew being cooked and hear the crew taking down the sail. The cabin boy is not feeling well. I think he's got something, he keeps sneezing.

The doctor's having a look at him now. The doctor says he has got something called a cold. Something bad happened today. One of my crew called 'Churchill' fell down the stairs and the doctor says he has a broken arm, he has bandaged it. I have a funny story for you.

The Indians of Brazil eat the flesh of their enemies. They cut a man up in pieces, which they put to dry in smoke. Every day they cut off a small piece and eat it with their normal food, to remember their enemies.

I have my own cabin to sleep in, so don't worry, I'll be safe. Hope that didn't scare you, I have to go, my tuna stew is ready, of course with sauerkraut and beef.

Oceans of love
Captain Skid
PS See you soon, write back as soon as possible.

Sadie Cole (10)
Brushwood Junior School

A Day In The Life Of A Tudor Sailor

HMS Cindaquil
Pacific Ocean
Southern Hemisphere
23rd May 1501

Dear Elizabeth 1,
I am writing a report on how I am doing on my voyage to the unknown. Please excuse my writing as the sea is very rough.

We are down to 100 sailors out of the 268 your majesty gave me. 50% of them died from typhoid, 25% from being thrown overboard in the awful storm that we had last night and the rest, unfortunately I didn't know about the swarm of rats which gnawed through almost every rope on deck!

We are just about to attack a ship which we think is Spanish, even from the distance I can tell. We can just about see, that it is piled high with gold and silver.

We have already been to Australia, with all the kangaroos and we are thinking about heading home after two years of sailing. Our food is very low and we are hoping there is food on the Spanish ship. I must go as the Spanish are starting to fire.

Yours sincerely

Captain Daygold

Amy Little (9)
Brushwood Junior School

A DAY IN THE LIFE OF A TUDOR SAILOR

HMS Eagle
The Eagle
The North Pole
23rd May 1501

Dearest Mother,

When we set off we all thought that we were heading for Africa but it turned out that we are going where no man's gone before!

The food is really bad, we have ship's biscuits, beef and we have to eat our sauerkraut.

Five men have already died in storms, which still is terribly sad. They lost their grip and fell overboard.

We captured a Portuguese ship on the 30th of January, there were ten treasure chests, five gallons of brandy and two cannons. We took them all including the ship.

Our fleet sailed on and we reached the most northern place, we called it The North Pole. It is really, really freezing because there are huge lumps of ice.

An officer was killed by a careless bowman when we were showing the natives our weapons. We all tried the man. He decided to be killed by the axe. It was another sad day, although he had been very careless.

On the 3rd of April, I was upgraded to an assistant captain as somebody else took poor old Johnny's place.

I have to end this letter now because a storm's brewing and I'm needed on deck, we're sailing south next. I'm thinking of you loads.

From your loving son
Pete

Joe Dixon (10)
Brushwood Junior School

A Day In The Life Of A Tudor Sailor

HMS Silver Dolphin
Equator
25th May 1515

Dear Family,

How are you? We have had an exhausting couple of weeks, finding the New World.

On our first week one of our best sailors came falling down from a broken rope and sadly died. The rest of the week went fine. We also discovered a place called the West Indies.

When we got there, we raided a ship called The Cyndaquil and got a lot of silver and gold.

Then during our second week, we had a terrible storm. The terrifying thunder was ripping our sail, tons of water pouring into our boat. It was awful. I'm now helping the carpenter make a new sail with some spare bits of material. The captain got extremely mad, because the ship's boy fell asleep whilst watching the hour glass. He now does the other jobs like the cleaning.

On our third and fourth week we discovered more land called Africa. We have lost 3 more people on the ship because they got attacked by Indians whilst exploring it. It was a very sad day. We have been through lots of terrible things but this was one of the worst, we got stuck on a reef and could not move for a long time but then luckily the wind changed direction and pushed us free.

I know this will take months to get to you, I might even be home by the time it's arrived, I'm missing you dearly.

Lots of love
James

Leah Pepper (10)
Brushwood Junior School

A Day In The Life Of A Tudor Sailor

HMS Gull
The Equator
15th May 1578

Dear Your Majesty, Queen Elizabeth,

We are sailing over the equator to where no man has gone before! I cannot tell you where we are exactly going, because we are going wherever the wind will take us. As you know we have been on this journey for 5 months.

We have just had a few miserable days, I will tell you now what happened. We had a traitor on board, he told Lord Burghley that we were going around the world and not to Alexandra. I knew he was a traitor because he tried to turn people against me. Following the rules of the sea we had to execute him.

As you might've known, we started off, at Plymouth, with 228 sailors, we now have 200 because we lost 28 of our finest sailors, that was another miserable day.

On the 15th of December 1577, we went on an island, called St Louie, the natives there were very kind indeed. They let us have some of their supplies, so we have plenty of good, they even crowned me King of St Louie! I said 'No' because I would never have given up my worthy crew!

This is a journey I will never ever forget.

Yours faithfully and truly
Captain Robs

Robyn Hughes (10)
Brushwood Junior School

A Day In The Life Of A Tudor Sailor

HMS Royal Discovery
25th May 1579

Dear Jamie,

The food here is low, no ale, only water, meat on Sunday and saukraut.
We also have a limited supply of ship's biscuits. My secret brandy (the
one below my bed) has been nicked by the lower cabins and they have
loads. All night I lie awake listening to them. One of their songs goes
like this: 'Who stays up way past midnight? Who drinks ale every
night? We do, we do. Who has brandy in the mouth? Who is sailing
further south? We are, we are!'

Anyway, most (but not all) people have no alcohol on the ship.

According to the hour glass, the date is 25th of May 1579. We're
having a heat wave here. I must end this letter now as I have lookout
duty.

From Alexander Howard

Alexander Howard (10)
Brushwood Junior School

A DAY IN THE LIFE OF A TUDOR SAILOR

HMS Eagle
25th May 1578

Dearest Mother,

At the moment we have been sailing through somewhere very hot, all the food is going smelly. We have had some thunderstorms and at one point, I thought the boat was going to be flooded when this wave hit. It was huge, about as tall as a house. Anyway, I've just been treated by the surgeon because in our last battle I got a bit of broken wood stuck in my leg but he said I'll be OK.

We have seen a few interesting things on our journey, like when we were somewhere cold, we found some black kind of bird, that doesn't really walk, they kind of waddle and they don't even fly, however, they swim well and taste nice. We have almost run out of ale. We have also made up this song to entertain us. It goes something like this:
'Who stays up drinking beer all night, we do, we do,' and so on. We have also been attacked by some viscious Indians apart from that, it has been fun.

Love from
Jamie.

Jamie Phipps (10)
Brushwood Junior School

A Day In The Life Of A Tudor Sailor

25th May 1578

Dear Elizabeth,

I am writing to tell you about a day on the HMS Eagle, 25th May 1578, a sad day for most of the crew, we ran out of ale, the crew have gone mad. Francis sent them to the hold for a rest.

We were attacked by some pirates from Spain, they took all the food and drink. This made the crew go nuts and pulled them down to get the beer, the Spanish put up a good fight, it was a bloody one, now we're down to 20 men out of 80.

Francis lost a hand, we lost 60 men and two ships of 5 ships, as I said, it was a very sad day.

Some good news, Francis and 10 men raided a town and got 2,000 gallons of ale, see you soon.

Love the cabin boy.

Calum Craig (10)
Brushwood Junior School

A Day In The Life Of Lynette Morgan

Hi it's me, Lynette Morgan. It's Tuesday today, I have to take Lee, Jake and Faye to school. It's very tiring. I told Lee to get up at 7o'clock today as I have to go to work early. I'll tell Lee to walk the rest of the way to school.

Every day I have to go to college and do lots of essays. I have to go to work and do more essays in a certain amount of time. You have to work for this for 3 years.

I'll go and pick Jake, Faye and Lee up from school and take Faye to ballet, then take Lee to Brownies. When I've picked Lee up from Brownies, I'll send them all to bed ready for Wednesday morning school.

Lee Morgan (8)
Brushwood Junior School

A Day In The Life Of A Ladybird

I am a ladybird. I am red with 8 black spots. I have two wings but you can't see them most of the time. My home is in the garden of 339 Berkhampsted Road in the garden by the big tree. I spend all day climbing up grass and leaves looking for insects to eat.

I am red and that warns other animals that I am not good to eat.

The people who let me live in their garden are very kind and if I am in danger, they move me and put me somewhere safe. I am kind to them because I eat the green flies that destroy their plants. Sometimes they take me into their house and look after me very carefully when it rains.

The three girls in the house come out and pick me up, then after a while they put me back. I tell all my relatives what fun I had.

Sidra Raja (10)
Brushwood Junior School

A Day In The Life Of A Cat

I'm a cat waiting to catch my prey, a juicy bird for lunch, my prey is on a tree ready to fall into my trap . . .

Got him! I've got to take it somewhere where nobody will find us. My favourite part of the bird is the breast part, it's so tender.

I'm ready to take a nap but I'm still hungry, I want another bird, beggars can't be choosers. I'm going to have a nap now.

James Hoisseini (11)
Brushwood Junior School

A Day In The Life Of A Bird

When night has faded and the sun has risen, I begin to flap my wings, then I take off and soar straight into the sky. I begin to search high and low for that juicy worm or the odd piece of bread.

I fly back to my nest with the things I've found, now I have to fly back and forth with the sticks and twigs to mend my nest.

I think that should be enough flying for today, so I think I'll settle down and go to sleep with my head tucked under my wing.

Lee Andrew Alan Sheppard (11)
Brushwood Junior School

A DAY IN THE LIFE OF AN ASTRONAUT

On Monday morning I went to my training session for three hours. I was so excited. In two days I am going to the moon, wow! It's like I can feel the gravity. I think I will say some special words.

The two days went by, I got to the rocket, in I went, I had to wait for half an hour.

20, 19, 18, I was counting myself, 17, 16, 15, the butterflies were in my stomach, 14, 13, 12, no stopping now, 11, 10, 9, 8, I could hear the crowd counting, 7, 6, 5, 4, 3, 2, 1, blast-off!

There was a slight shake, the rocket went higher and higher, all I could see was tiny black dots. I could only see moving cars, lorries and buses. I was so excited, going to the moon. I had reached the moon, I could see huge craters as big as the volcanoes on Earth.

When I got to the moon, I could see our Earth in the distance, I was walking on the moon and I said, 'The eagle has landed,' and 'This is one small step for a man, and one giant leap for mankind.'

I was walking on the moon and when I was walking on the moon, I thought it was like you could walk to the other end of the moon.

Maybe some day I will go back to the moon again.

Matthew O'Mahony (9)
Brushwood Junior School

A Day In The Life Of A Frog

Hi, I'm a frog, I live in a lake, I'm under the water, I am trying to sleep but it's cold, misty and cold, oh there are humans, dive, dive, they are putting their hand in. They're taking the frogspawn out.

Crunch! 'Oh, that frog bit me,'

'I don't believe you, ouch, he bit me too.'

'Mummy!' the boys screamed, then loads of frogs appeared and one of the frogs asked the boy, 'What's your name?'

'Scott, hip hip hooray, hip hip hooray,' I become king of the frogs I got loads of waterworms, snails, flies, dragonflies and got a lovely place to sleep.

Nicholas Bunce (9)
Brushwood Junior School

A Day In The Life Of A T-Rex

I hate eating meat, I really should be looking after the other dinosaurs, but that's what I do. Well I am on an island, but I forgot what this island is called because I am always thinking about meat.

I don't even want to think about meat but my wife does want me to eat meat but I don't like those Anklosauruses they always swing their tails at me.

Oh oh! My wife is coming roooaaarrr!
'I've got meat for you.'
'Oh no! I don't want meat.'
'Why darling you always want it,'
'I don't,'
'Well you have to okay!'
'I am going to round the island OK and find my own food.'

Well this island has got lots of coconut trees and one volcano. Oh no, it's an Anklosaurus oh no, I better run. What! Oh roar stegasarus, I want to get off this island, I will give up all right, I give up. I am sorry, I will push, try to grass or something else, no I will push you down the hole. Oh I think I missed something else, we have holes as well and we have a quick sand pit. This will be my end ah! Boom! Yes we did it, we killed T-Rex.

Jamie Winfield (9)
Brushwood Junior School

A Day In The Life Of Elizabeth

I am so lonely, I don't have any friends to play with. It's not fair, I wrote a letter and the guard read it because he had to, but the letter was very naughty. So the guard didn't send it. The guard went somewhere and they left the gun there, there was no one else in the house so I shot one of the guards and the guard became a ghost. It was so funny because he had spiky hair and he had a pointed nose and his ears were like Dumbo and he looked very funny.

No one visits me so that's why I am so lonely. My dad gave me a little money just to buy books because I liked reading and learning so that's why I bought books. Whenever I write a letter, the guard has to read it, then he can send it. If someone writes a letter to me, the guard has to read it, then he can give it to me.

I am scared and frightened because I know that my father had my mother beheaded. My mother, Anne Boolean did nothing wrong. I'm scared in case Henry decides to behead me to stop me being queen.

Tabasum Zulfiqar (9)
Brushwood Junior School

A DAY IN THE LIFE OF A FOX

The fox slipped quietly out of the tyre heap on a mission, looking for food for the vixen. The vixen was currently looking after the newborn cubs. The fox was going to get the chicken that he saw at the farm through the woods and over the road and over the wire fence.

The farmer didn't take too kindly to this as it was his livelihood. The fox slipped under the wire into the farm. He approached a hut and was padding up the ramp, when he saw the plump chicken. He pounced, hit and bit into the neck, and the chicken went limp. The chickens clucked at this red intruder but the fox ignored this and dragged out the dead chicken. Now there seemed nothing to stop him, but the farmer was roused by the clucking and he saw the red intruder and fired his shotgun.

'Oi you! Get off my land and my chickens.' He fired again twice. The fox put the chicken on his back and ran. He ran across the road, that to his knowledge wasn't used. But this day he was wrong. A car roared around the bend doing well over 40. The fox stared at the car, too frightened to move. The drive of the car skidded, just missing the fox.

The fox ran on. The driver, his car wrecked and smoking, got out and cursed the fox but the fox ran on, just missing a tree that was being felled. Back to his family, the vixen and the tyre heap.

Alex Parry-Jones (11)
Brushwood Junior School

A DAY IN THE LIFE OF FELIX THE CAT

7.00am   I felt a bit of a nudge, it woke me up. It was that Catherine girl, she'd woken me up. Oh well, that's my day started, I'll just have a stretch and a quick cat lick and creep downstairs and see if they have left me any food out in the kitchen. That hamster in the brother's room looks tasty, but I think I will get told off if I try and eat it.

7.30am   Once I got downstairs, I had a good old scratch at the carpet, walked round the dog, then strolled into the kitchen to see what was there. I was in luck, they had left me some food. Good job the dog hadn't eaten it. In my bowl was my favourite flavoured cat food. It was chicken and gravy. Once I'd had enough, I felt I had to go out. Whose garden should I choose today?

8.00am   I dived through the cat flap into the garden. It was a sunny morning with no clouds in the sky and there were lots of birds singing in the trees. Yum, yum I thought to myself. I decided I would catch a mouse today. The best place to look is in the hedge across the road, but I will have to be careful crossing that busy road, some of my friends have crossed it and never come back.

9.00am   I'm safely across. I can't hear any mice but if I lie quiet and very still, it might be my lucky day.

10.00am   I suddenly hear a sound, and get myself ready to pounce. I kept my body low and in a flash I leapt into the air and captured the mouse in my paws.

11.00am   After all that excitement I felt I needed a cat nap. It started to rain so I definitely went in. When I went through the cat flap I was dripping wet and I left dirty black footprints on the kitchen floor. I decided to sleep on Catherine's bed. I snuggled in-between the soft toys and went to sleep.

5.00pm   I eventually woke up after a long sleep. It's a hard life being a cat. I stretched out, dug my claws into the duvet and had a good scratch.
I heard some activity going on downstairs, I could smell food cooking and hear pots and pans. That must mean 'tea time'. I wandered downstairs and saw the mum standing in the kitchen. I rubbed my head against her legs to try to persuade her to feed me. Sometimes it takes a while for her to notice me. If I weave in and out of her legs, she will definitely feed me because she won't want to trip over me.

6.00pm   I am now full, I've had my tea and stroll round the garden. It's stopped raining but I like this part of the day because I can go and curl up on someone's lap. They sit in a big chair in front of a big box that lights up for quite a long time and and they always stroke me. It's a hard life being a cat.

11.00pm   The big people have gone to bed now and all I have to do is to find a comfy spot on one of the beds to go to sleep on. It's a hard life being a cat!

Catherine Ball (11)
Brushwood Junior School

A Day In The Life Of A Pet Goldfish

Woke up this morning because those big fat things with no fins were crashing around. They were spraying water around as usual.

Food was dropped into my tank some time later and I gobbled it up quickly. I wish they'd give me more. I'm always hungry and it doesn't help when they don't feed me.

The things are doing something called 'bedfast' they do this every day. They often complain about 'getting up to lay bedfast.'

Today there is a lot of noise coming from a place they call 'kitkin'. They are making banging and crashing noises. I've only been to the kitkin a few times, but I don't mind. I'll go back to sleep and start the day when they've gone.

Now they've gone I can start the day properly, I think I'll swim around the tank then dig in the gravel for food.

Ouch, damn! One of the big things has caught me in a plastic cup. They're tipping the water out of my tank. Now they're rubbing it with a 'cloff'. Now they're pouring water back in, can't think why they've bothered to tip it out in the first place!

Well I guess I can go back to sleep now for the night. Bye.

Alexis Ellender (10)
Brushwood Junior School

A Day In The Life Of Kate In World War II

Today I was woken up at 8 o'clock due to an air raid siren, then a gas mask was thrown at me by my brother. I put it on and my brother, dad and I ran to the air raid shelter. In the air raid shelter there were four bunk beds, some games, guns for protection and some food.

The air raid lasted for an hour, but there weren't any bombs dropped on the village. Then the Air Raid Warden came and said 'There might be some poisoned gas around, so you should keep your gas masks on for an hour.' It was Sunday and it was ration day, we went to the shops but when we came out we were stopped by soldiers and asked to show our Identity Cards (this was normal) then after lunch we had to go to school because there were evacuees there and dad had to choose some children. Dad chose a girl and a boy, they were called Victoria and Jake. Then we went home for tea and we played a game which I won, but only narrowly because Victoria came second. Then there was the air raid siren and we grabbed our gas masks and ran to the shelter again.

It lasted for two hours and a bomb was dropped on the village, but no one was hurt.

Isobel Wright (11)
Brushwood Junior School

A DAY IN THE LIFE OF A CALF

Thud! Thud! Thud! I was in a stupor, half conscious and dazed. Suddenly I heard footsteps coming towards me. A man shouted *'Huh! There's a calf alive!'*

I cuddled up to my mother and found that she was unnaturally cold and stiff. I then looked up to find that she was dead. As I realised this, I felt as if everything in life had vanished and there was no point in living, since the one person I had loved most had been killed.

I thought no one else cared for me, and I struggled to get up on my feet but my legs felt like jelly. As I staggered and fell down, a pair of gentle hands lifted me and I looked up and saw my owner Board. By his side was Michaela anxiously looking down at me. They carried me to a straw-lined garage behind their yellow bungalow and laid me gently and carefully on the straw.

I was feeling very tired and weak, but Michaela and her son Ross took turns to bottle-feed me and pamper me. From their conversation I got to know that I had been found alive by the man who came to disinfect the carcasses. Then I recollected everything that had happened on that farm.

I was born at Clarence Farm, which is run by Michaela Board. I was looked after by her very well, but I could remember how one day, all of a sudden, I was taken with the others to a place away from the farm because they had found out that there was a case of foot-and-mouth at a neighbouring farm. I didn't know what happened until later. Now I wonder what is going to happen to me?

MAFF vets came to see me. They were determined to put me down. Oh God, what am I to do? Will they again give the order to kill me? In that case of course it would have been better off if they had killed me with my beloved mother. Why should I undergo such agony?

After their visit in the morning, the MAFF officials arrived at the farm again in the afternoon. They were discussing amongst themselves about the next step to take. Ah, poor me! Why should this happen to me? Now that I have been cared for so much by my owners, I wish to live with them although I longed and yearned for my beloved mother. They examined me for symptoms of foot-and-mouth. Luckily I didn't have any. Michaela said that she would not allow them to come and see me anymore other than inspecting me for that horrible disease. When I heard this I was greatly relieved. I hated them. Oh! I hate the sight of them more, because they killed my mother. It is because of the mistake of all these officials that I suffered greatly. I was hungry, thirsty and traumatised. I shiver to think of it again.

To my utmost happiness, I heard Michaela saying that I would be growing up and was going to be a companion for the pony called Teddy. I would be having as much grass as I could eat and going to have a good life.

Towards the evening people around my farm came to see me as they had come to know I had escaped death. Photographers came to take photos of me to publish in their respective papers.

Since I have survived for five days after starving and being under a pile of cattle and sheep slaughtered because of the foot-and-mouth- cull policy, I was given the name Phoenix, I am very proud of this and I am grateful to my owners Board, Michaela and their son Ross for giving me a new lease of life.

Sathia Narayana Navaneetham (10)
Brushwood Junior School

A DAY IN THE LIFE OF A ROMAN SOLDIER

Every day I wake up, the first task is to get dressed into my armour. When I first became a Roman solider, it took me forever to fit into the rigid metal chest-plate. But after six months in the Legion, it doesn't take me half as long.

Next I must eat. I must eat the vile repulsive food the General calls porridge, I think it's poison. One of my comrades told me to hold my nose whilst eating to hide the flavour, but that didn't work, so I just swallow it down as quickly as possible.

As soon as I finish I must leave for training with my comrades. We must march to the training camp in exact straight lines, holding our pikes as still as rocks.

Our training consists of duelling with wooden swords, practising hand-to-hand combat. Learning tactical manoeuvres, using siege weapons for target practice and marching 1000 paces, also carrying extremely heavy bags, did I mention they're full of rocks?

Many soldiers have died from the sheer intensity and pressure of our training. I feel great remorse for their departed souls.

After hours of training, my comrades and I return to our campsite where thousands of tents lie cramped together.

Everyday my fellow soldiers have different dreams, but I always have the same dream. . . of becoming a Centurion.

Javed Ahmed (10)
Brushwood Junior School

A DAY IN THE LIFE OF A HAMSTER

As my little Stella runs around her cage, she looks up at me and runs into her house with a chimney on top. Then all I can see is her little pink nose and her glistening brown eyes.

Then I do not see her until my bedtime because she does not come out unless it is dark and quiet. When she does come out she thinks she can run faster than Michael Schumacher on the Silverstone race track.

She has two cages, one big one and one small one. The big one has a treehouse, the other one has a wheel. In the treehouse she has chocolate drops, they are little bits of chocolate for hamsters.

I check to see if her bedding is clean. I have had her for two and a half years.

So that is the day of the life of my hamster.

Christopher Newton (10)
Brushwood Junior School

A DAY IN THE LIFE OF A HAMSTER

Snowflake scrumbles and scrambles in his little house, that is if he can fit into it. His little pink nose and his shining red eyes poke out of his little window, sniffing the nice cool air.

His little legs take him everywhere, when he thinks that he can run faster than Mika Hakkinen in the Australian Grand Prix. He comes out when you are least expecting him to.

Snowflake always wants to come out to play but sometimes we can't get him out because we are doing something else. But snowflake is the best pet you could ever think of having.

Oliver Piested (11)
Brushwood Junior School

A Day In The Life Of An Owl

Waking up from a good days sleep Tawny the owl instantly thought of food.

Swooping down from his branch in the old oak like an aeroplane closing in on the enemy and . . . wham! The first unexpected and most probably unwilling victim of the night.

It was a shrew. Until Tawny pierced his sharp claws into its body, making it a *deceased shrew*.

Tawny glided gracefully into the night back to his branch in the old oak tree. 'Tu-whit; Tu-whoo!' Tawney's sharp cry broke the quiet of the night and acted like an alarm bell to all the small mammals who were sent shuffling and rustling into the dark wood. 'Great!' Tawny thought, 'it's gonna be harder than ever to get some grub now!'

As Tawny jumped off his perch for the second time, he heard something and using his excellent eyesight he scanned the ground and amongst the dead leaves saw something was moving.

His feathers allowed him to fly unbelievably silently, he stalked his prey and pounced! It was a vole 'That'll do for the night.' Tawny said in a cheery voice and then soared towards his branch in the old oak tree.

Ben Rivans (11)
Brushwood Junior School

A Day In The Life Of Heather

On September 3rd 1939, England declared war on Germany prior to Neville Chamberlain, Heather's father, the British Prime Minister, going to Germany to sign a Peace Treaty with Adolf Hitler.

I got up in the morning and saw that my father wasn't at the dinner table.
'Mother, where's father?' I asked, wondering where he could be.
'He has gone to Germany for a day or two. He'll be back soon. Now go upstairs and get ready, you need to go and work at the farm today.'

I ran up the stairs and got ready with a blink of an eye.

As soon as I got to the farm, I started milking the cows one by one until all twenty-nine were milked. After I had milked all the cows, it was almost time for lunch and today I had my favourite sandwiches, pickle and cheese.

After lunch I needed to start with the chickens, they were running all over the place. Eventually I had finished with the chickens and then I met up with my best friend, Elizabeth. After talking to Elizabeth I asked Mr Jones if I could go home. He said I'd worked so hard that he hoped I had enough energy left for tomorrow.

As soon as I got home I started writing in my diary:

Dear Diary

I went to the farm today. It was a lot of hard work. Well harder than I thought anyway and I feel terrible. I have a weird feeling when father comes back from Germany he's going to be very angry. I wonder why? Maybe because Germany will try to attack us. That will be terrible, we'll need to carry those gas masks, the horrible ones and we won't be able to have a lot of fun. Well there's not much I can write today apart from that I still have a crush on Julius. He noticed me on the farm. I feel absolutely great. I wish he'd ask me to go somewhere with him. It would be like a date.

Heather

After writing my diary, I asked Mother if I could take a quick shower because I was worn out after working on the farm. Later, in the evening, Father came back from Germany and he was in a terrible mood, as I suspected he would be. He went to the study with Mother and I overheard them speaking about Germany. They are going to attack us - how terrible! Father pressed the siren and everyone was aware, we never thought another war would actually happen.

Later that evening Father had a meeting with everyone, we all had to wear gasmasks and make weapons. I was to be evacuated with all the other children and we were to be separated from our parents.

That night I could not sleep. I kept wondering about what would happen. How would life be without my parents? I could not possibly imagine living without them. Life would be unbearable, I wondered how I would cope. Then a little while later I drifted off to another land.

Sameera Yasin (10)
Brushwood Junior School

A DAY IN THE LIFE OF A ROMAN SOLDIER

I got up this morning to a repulsive smell. I sniffed around wondering what it was. I stepped outside my tent to see cook making breakfast. I quickly ran back into my tent and zipped it up unable to bear the vile smell a second longer. I got dressed inside my tent, I put my helmet on and marched off to join my Legion. I met them in a deadly straight line with the General at the front. We sat down at the enormous breakfast table after five minutes of marching. The cook served us . . . porridge.. Lumpy porridge. Mouldy porridge. Gone-off porridge. I held my nose as I swallowed the vile goo. At last, when breakfast had finished, we went to our daily training. We started off by duelling with each other with wooden swords. I am particularly good at this and I defeated everybody else in my group. Next we fought our Centurions one at a time. I was knocked unconscious by his stunning blow. When I came to in the medical tent, I was sent straight back out to train. Our Centurion flung a bag of rocks over my back and said I was to walk 1000 paces before returning to camp for lunch.

When lunch had finished (which was corn, bacon and cheese mixed together) most of the Legion returned to their tents to read a book or do something else. Suddenly the alarm bell went off, every man in the army knew what that meant. We were under attack! The ten Centurions who were in charge of us were firing orders at the Legion. Men gathered in groups behind siege catapults. I was sent to fight with my trusty sword, I slayed a few people before having to retreat as war elephants marched over the horizon.

I wasn't quite sure what happened after that, when I looked up I saw dead bodies everywhere including our own. Our seven Centurions announced that we had been lowered to 678 men. He said we should repair the dinner hall, which had been very badly damaged. My task was to replenish some of the broken planks. By dinner, we had finished and celebrated with a succulent luxurious dinner.

When I got back to my tent I fell asleep, dreaming my biggest dream which was to become a Centurion.

Robert Gholam (11)
Brushwood Junior School

A DAY IN THE LIFE OF A HAMSTER

I like being a hamster because you get to run around in the plastic balls and you get to run around in the wheel too. You don't have to go to school and you can sleep in bed all day.

I get to eat when I want to and I can go round in the tunnels, it is really dark and I play every half an hour. The food is quite nice and I really like the sunflower seeds.

I have a water bottle. My owner takes me out of my cage. He puts me in a ball and lets me run around. it's really fun!

Jamie Walker (11)
Brushwood Junior School

A DAY IN THE LIFE OF A TUDOR SAILOR

The Endeavour
Plymouth
1519 January 3rd

Dearest Moiter

6am: I'm just about to set sail on Magellon's ship. The ship looks like it's in good condition. We are travelling round the world, it should take three years. The deck is spotlessly clean and the Endeavour carries 40 guns and 12 cannons. The food is going to rot if the food comes into contact with the air, the meat is salted. We have a good chance of getting diseases like scurvy. We will be setting off in stormy weather. We are now setting sail.

7am: We are sailing through the Atlantic Ocean. We have met an English ship called the Warrior, they carry 43 guns and 4 cannons. I have started to get scurvy. We have killed 2 seals and 30 fishes. We are going to stop in India, the Endeavour will take 4 men and 4 guns and the Warrior will take 12 men and 12 guns. We are meeting outside an Indian village.

Today my jobs are to climb the rigging to the crows nest and clean the deck with a scrubbing brush. Later on my jobs are to watch the half hour glass then call up to the captain who will mark it down then turn it over. We will be eating on the floor or in the ship if the weather is bad and we are sleeping on the deck if the weather is bad, we will be sleeping in the ship. Sorry I have to end this letter, I have to clean the deck. I miss you.

From your dearest son
    Liam Ryan Berger
        xxx xxx xxx xxx

Liam Berger (10)
Brushwood Junior School

A DAY IN THE LIFE OF A TUDOR SAILOR
(The Elizabeth, somewhere in The Atlantic Ocean, 15 October 1579)

Dearest Mother,

Today I feel awful about leaving you by yourself and I feel the same with my friends, because it will be about 2-4 years before I come home.

The food on The Elizabeth is not quite what I expected but it's better than nothing. I clean the floor. I mostly do everything. If I'm protected from dangers I'll be very grateful and hopefully the weather will be fine.

Today we are going to a tropical island where we are going to find some treasure which will be all gold and silver. Gold as the sun and silver as the moon reflecting in calm water. Afterwards I will do some work. I'll watch the hourglass. After I've washed the deck with a scrubbing brush, I'll clean the filthy food pots which have maggots in. I'll then climb the rigging into the crow's nest.

Oh by the way, do you miss me, because I miss you!

From your loving son Carl.

Caryl Morgan (10)
Brushwood Junior School

A Day In The Life Of Ozzy The Parrot

(Ozzy our pet parrot (written through Ozzy's eyes)

I am a Senegal parrot and my day begins at 7.45am when Ashley's mum pulls the cover off my cage and Ashley starts speaking to me. Then they have breakfast and next they go upstairs and leave me. Shortly they all come back downstairs wearing different clothes, then they turn on the radio and go to a place called school.

Mum returns ten minutes later and starts clearing up. She lets me out around 9.15am. I get really excited at being out of my cage and I can stretch my wings and fly around. Mum gives me lots of cuddles and kisses. I try to talk back but I can only make squeaking noises at the moment. I hope that I can soon talk back to them. I sometimes sit on her shoulder and I nibble at the duster or I sit on the hoover for a ride. She gives me some grapes or a banana to eat which I love. I'm out for about 45 minutes then she puts me back in my cage. I play with my toys for a while then I get tired so I have a nap.

Before long she goes out again and comes in with Ashley and Matthew. I get really excited to see them. When it's dark I am out and flying around again and everyone plays with me. Dad puts clean food and water out for me and fresh fruit and veg.

Very soon it's time for bed and they put me back into the cage and cover it over. Goodnight!

Ashley Morgan (10)
Madley Primary School

A DAY IN THE LIFE OF HENRY VIII

If you think about it Henry VIII was quite a weird person. I mean, six wives! Do you know anybody with six wives? No I didn't think so. Do you want to know the names of the six wives and how Henry managed six wives? OK here they are, yes and how he managed them all:

Catherine Of Aragon got divorced, Anne Boleyn got beheaded, Jane Seymour died of sickness, Anne Of Cleves got divorced, Catherine Howard got beheaded and last of all Katherine Parr outlived Henry.

Henry VIII wore very strong armour. This armour took a lot of work to make. If you want to hear about how much work went into it, keep reading.

Hours and hours were spent making Henry's armour. I mean there was measuring, moulding, cutting, hammering and then starting all over again. OK, OK, so that isn't really weird but at least it's a fact.

This is the really weird bit. You see, Henry killed thousands and thousands of birds each year but when he saw one dying in his back garden he burst out crying.

Now back to his wives. Do you know why Anne Boleyn got beheaded? Yes, fine, fine by me! Now how should I put it. She gave birth to a girl but Henry wanted a boy (quite a stupid reason to be beheaded). When she was killed, Henry went off and he got another wife.

Robyn Barratt (8)
Madley Primary School

A DAY IN THE LIFE OF MY MUM

In the morning my mum has to wake everybody up. Once we have finished our breakfast she does the washing up for us.

My mum is pregnant so she says, 'Could you pick this up for me?' She has to take us to school and then go to work where she cooks in the kitchen. At three o'clock she waits for us and then brings us home.

She child-minds people and makes food for them. Sometimes when she is child-minding she gets angry becasue the children won't do as she says and she has to tell them off. When they go home she clears up and starts to do the washing up.

After the children have gone she then sits down and has a rest. After she's had a rest she watches TV and says to me, 'Come and sit by me!' She then lights a fire to keep us warm. She also lets me go outside to play with my friends. Sometimes she lets us watch scary movies. She watches a lot of scary movies. Sometimes she listens to music. She laughs a lot because my dad makes her. Then she say that I have to go to bed. She kisses me, my brothers and sister goodnight.

Sarah Guy (8)
Madley Primary School

A Day In The Life Of Rolf Harris

On the 30th April 2001 I took my hamster Milly to the animal hospital because he was ill. Rolf Harris, the vet and the nurse treated Milly for sticky eyes and at the same time cut his nails.

After Rolf had helped treat Milly, he asked if I would like to stay with him for the day. I then rang my mum to come and take Milly home. When Milly had gone we started practising to be on television, but in the middle there was a real emergency. I went with Rolf to find out what it was. It was a puppy stuck in the mud with a broken leg. Ten minutes later the fire engines and also the police arrived. The fire-fighters had to get some rope and tie it to the puppy and pull at the other end. When we finally got her out, we thought of three names, Jess, Becky and Bonnie. We selected Jess. We also had to name some other animals. They were gerbils and we called them Bill and Ben.

Later that day Rolf appealed on television for homes for the puppy and the gerbils. This was the end of my day at the studio but I heard a week later that the puppy and the gerbils had found new homes, thanks to Rolf.

Emma Butler (10)
Madley Primary School

A DOG'S LIFE

Hello, my name's Rolo. I'm going to tell you what I do in a day. I wake up and look around and if there's no one up yet I go on the sofa but I have to make sure they don't see me. When they come down I pretend to greet them and then go back to my basket until they finish breakfast. I then pester them until they take me on a walk.

When I get home I have my breakfast then I hop in my basket until they go to work. Then I go on the sofa or talk to Toby, (next door's dog). I say it's so unfair we're not allowed to go upstairs and we don't have a proper bed. After cursing a few times we go chasing sheep around the orchard and Toby pretends to be a commentator of a horse race.

When I get home I am just in time because Sylvia has just got back. When Matthew, Nathan and Megan get back they play with me but when they watch TV I pull everything out of the bin. After tea they go upstairs so I hop on the sofa and shut my eyes tight.

Matthew Hancox (10)
Madley Primary School

A DAY IN THE LIFE OF MATTHEW JONES' DUMPER

A friend of mine asked me if I wanted a dumper truck (a very old dumper). I was not sure so I asked my dad. He thought about it and said yes I could have it. It was Sunday morning so my dad and I went to fetch the dumper with my dad's (Manitou ??). My dad took the dumper to my grandad's farm. We tried starting it but it would not go.

The next weekend we changed the rods on the steering and did some other maintenance work on the dumper. My grandad came with the tractor and towed my dad along with a piece of rope. The dumper started to go. We had to have two new tyres and we wire-brushed the paintwork down and then painted it yellow.

A few days later it as my eighth birthday and my mum took, Bill, John, Matthew, Morgan and me to MacDonald's for tea. After tea we went to the farm and my dad was home from work early. We were allowed to get on the dumper and he let us take it in turns to drive it. My friends said they had a great time on the dumper. They then all went home happily. (I can't wait until the summer holidays!).

Matthew Jones (9)
Madley Primary School

A DAY IN THE LIFE OF TOFFEE BOLTON

One hot summer day, I woke up at 6 o'clock and felt rather peckish. I had a good stretch and a bit of a scratch before I went and trampled all over my wonderful owners.

When we got downstairs they fed me my most favourite breakfast which was crunch biscuits and nice soft chicken meat. After breakfast I needed a bit of a stroll so I stood and shouted by the door so that my owners let me out. It was a beautiful day so I trotted down the garden path to meet my friend.

I popped next door to see Kitty, she's my girlfriend. We decided to go and catch some fish. The fish were a lot of fun but while we were fishing Kitty's owner's dog shocked us and we fell into the pond. I had to save Kitty and then we ran like mad to get away.

We ran into the cornfield to play our best game, Catch A Mouse If You Can. The rules of the game are: 1 stay as still and as quiet as you can, 2 wait while the mice come out to play, 3 chase them all away.

Kitty and I had a great time. We only stopped playing when my owner called me. We said we'd do it all again tomorrow and said our goodbyes and left.

Alexandra Bolton (8)
Madley Primary School

A DAY IN THE LIFE OF MY DAD

My dad has to get up at 6.30am and has to leave for work at 7.30am.

My dad is a business development director at a company called Gyrus Medical. His office is in Cardiff and he normally arrives there at 8.30am. The first thing he does when he arrives is to check his mail and e-mail. Then he has a Project Progress Meeting with the engineers that make things for him. Then Dad has to talk to lawyers about business opportunities, then he has lunch at 1.00pm but he only eats fruit because he's on a diet! After lunch he has conference calls with American colleagues.

My dad often has to travel to America so he has to phone the States to organise his next trips. Dad has to talk to the managing director and chairman every day to organise meetings with other colleagues. He has to write reports on everything he's done and make suggestions to the management team on which direction their business should go.

When he's done all that, Dad shuts down his computer, tidies up all the paper on his desk and posts any letters into the out-tray. Then he locks his office door, says goodbye to anyone who's still there and if there is no one there, sets the office alarm and locks the door. He then gets in his car and drives home, getting petrol on the way if he needs it.

Alexander Fraser (9)
Madley Primary School

BLACKBEARD'S DIARY

5.30am 'Avast there! Where's me grog? Pass some meat, I'm starving!'
Ship's biscuit, too. Mmmm! Lovely!

6.30am 'All hands on deck! You there, shoot that seagull, it'll do nicely
for me. Lunch! Forgot to clean the deck. Then see what me cutlass can
do! *Splash!* Ahh! Music to me ears!'

7.00am 'Who rules the sea?'
'Blackbeard!'
'Yes, good, good! Carry on with your chores.'

8.30am Yaaawn! I'm fed up of playing snap. I think I'll sharpen me
cutlass.
'You, Smee, on guard! Hy-yah! Whoa! Yah! Uuurrrgh!'
Thump! Hmmm, I think I need another opponent to practise with!

11.00am 'Food! Fetch me food!'
Gulp!
'Lovely! I do like roasted seagull!'

12.30pm Oh oh! Soldiers!
'Sir! Shall I - uuurgh!'
Whump! *Oh darn!* That was one of my best men!
'Attack! they shall not take this ship, the Jolly Jack!'
Bang! Ow! My leg!

5.00pm My wooden leg feels nice!

9.30pm *Snore! Crack!* Oh bum, my hammock broke!

David Newstead (10)
Morgans Primary School

A SHORT DAY FOR DERIK

I am miserable, I am fat and now I am divorced. I knew this day would come, Derik divorced, per! I might as well kill myself. I am twenty-nine, nothing, no job, no wife, just a son . . . ow yeah a son that hates his mother, where's my . . . my . . . arhh phone 12726578101 ring ring

'Hello, it's Snake, who are ya?'

'It's ya dad.'

'Oh what do you want?'

'Well, I am in town and . . . um ya mum divorced me!'

'*Cool.*'

'Shut up! Anyway you know ya got dat rifle. Come and help me. Meet me at Woolies 1pm *with* the gun.'

'OK bye.'

Perfect me and my son are gonna kill Sue . . .

'Hey Snake, she's in Tesco's. We got a ladder, now let's get on the roof . . . a perfect hit, she's there looking at the chips. Shoot her in the head *then* and only *then* I will lower ya down, then shoot her in the heart. *Go!*'

Bang! . . . sss . . . sss *Bang!*

'*Run* quickly . . . come on *split!*'

'Where was it chief?'

'FBI guy was in Tesco's. He went to the mounds.'

'OK got ta go.'

'Hey, Snake the cops are gonna see us soon and capture us so let's split up, I'll go right.'

'Bye Dad.'

'Bye Son.'

'*Wait there.* I believe your name's Snake.'

'Um yes Sir, guy, person, cop.'

'*Shut up!* You're coming with us. You're gonna have a life in prison, ha!'

'*No! Dad! Dad! Daaaad! I'm only twelve!*'

'Who was that? Oh my god it's a helicopter!'
'Stand with your hands up.'
'Never!'
There's a cliff . . . gulp . . .
Don't Jump!'
'Aaaaahhhhh!'

Tobi Martin (10)
Morgans Primary School

A DAY IN THE LIFE OF BOB THE BUILDER

'Right gang, let's get to work,' said Bob.

'Right,' shouted the gang.

The gang was made up of five machines. Scoop, Muck, Dizzy, Rolly and Lofty.

'Let's make an early start 'cause we've got a lot of work to do today.'

'Right, all of you sort out who's going to start mixing the cement and who's doing whatever else.'

'All right,' said Muck. 'I'll do the mixing cement, that's what I'm good at.'

'Right, I'll need a hand with putting the bricks on,' Bob shouted. 'Scoop, come over here and help me.'

'Alright Boss.'

Muck spread the cement on, Scoop lifted the bricks to Lofty and Rolly, gave them to Bob whilst Dizzy was putting windows in.

'Last few bricks,' shouted Bob down to Lofty.

'Bob watch out,' they shouted.

Bob fell down off the roof straight into the muddy sand. Bob didn't find it amusing but the rest of the gang did.

'Ha . . . ha ha ha . . . ha,' they laughed.

'Anyway, gang why are you laughing when we have to put this all back up again?'

'*Oh no,*' said the gang.

'Not laughing any more, hey,' laughed Bob.

After a hard day's work of putting up the building again they had time for a mud fight.

'Ah, take this Bob,' shouted Scoop.

'Take this,' shouted Lofty.

After a great mud fight it was home and to bed.
'Well, a good day's work,' Bob said to himself.

That night the building which he had just built fell down because of the storm and cracked a hole in the roof. Whoops! Another job for Bob the Builder tomorrow!

Michael Dunnage (10)
Morgans Primary School

A Day In The Life Of Kimball O'Hara (Kim By Rudyard Kipling)

'Ayah! It is too early to wake up, washerwoman! Let us be, for we are weary still of yesterday. Our feet need rest, for we walked but ten miles yesterday. Let us be I say! Alas! She is right, look into the sky, see how high the sun is, disciple, we must be getting on to Lahore City! Greetings, washerwoman, let your kindness be rewarded for letting us stay for the night, thank you, and thank you again for your kindness. Come disciple, we must find the Red Bull, and you, O man of Buddha, must find the River of the Arrow.'

'I agree, little Kim,' forced out a weary and tired, very tired, Buddhist monk, who was Kim's best friend and only companion, on his quest to find the Red Bull on the green field.

The monk's goal, however was to find the river where the arrow that the great Buddha shot, landed. He was seeking redemption from the wheel of life.

'Yes, yes, Kim, but if we are going we must hurry, for Lahore is a day's quick walk from here, and you said you wanted to be there, in Lahore, before dusk.'

'Come, come, then disciple, the washerwoman has gone, and we have no money,' hurried Kim.

'Be gone, then Kim' said the monk 'I will follow thee soon. I have some business to attend to here.'

'Fine then, but hurry, disciple. I wish to be in Lahore with thee, not alone,' stated Kim.

Kim hurried off with a puzzled look on his face, in the direction of Lahore. Kim was baffled as to why his disciple had left him, Kim, to carry on alone. Anyway, Kim hurried on, anxious to be in Lahore before nightfall. Kim was making good time towards Lahore, and he thought he should have been there well before nightfall, so he started singing. Kim was on top of the world, he was very happy, when he came to a T-junction. Coming from the left were white men, white soldiers, with guns. Kim didn't know what to do. His father had been a soldier, so they may accept him. On the other hand, having lived in India for so long, Kim didn't look like a Sahib at all. Kim really didn't know what to do . . .

William Brady (10)
Morgans Primary School

A DAY IN THE LIFE OF A PEN

Jimmy Palmers was being carefully produced in the main factory of Berõl handwriting pens on the corner of Trafalgar Square, London. What a privilege for an average pen to be made in their company's main factory. Jimmy was the 368,000th pen exactly to be made. He was hurried along the machine for recycling pieces, past the ladies and men constructing pens and straight to the final detail department. He had no reason to be placed in the placing together department because he had been put together by other pens' pieces. Shiny pieces. After around thirty minutes of paint and final detail put on him, Jimmy was rushed into a box with eight other pens. After around five minutes had gone, they were in a truck heading to a school in Hertford. Jimmy was probably the best pen in there, with his shiny paint and smooth detail, all the other pens were amazed at him. They told him that they were travelling to a school named Morgans JMI. It was bumpy in the back. Next minute they were being unloaded by the caretaker to a Y5 class. They were talking about how they die and things like that. But humans can never hear these pens talking because when they talk it's like a tiny little whisper as loud as the scurrying feet on a mouse. A few seconds later they were inside the class drawer of pens. It wasn't until 11.00 that Jimmy was used. For English, apparently pens have the personalities of their users. So Jimmy was questioning, sometimes scared, tall, enthusiastic and an excellent pen. In English he chatted to his fellow pens again about death and how you can die. Everybody loved him so much he had been completely used by 3.20. The children thought he was so cool and he was really shiny and had fantastic detail! But at 3.20 came the time he had dreaded. Death! Jimmy ran out of ink and toppled hard onto the floor and his hollow body smashed. There lay the greatest pen that had ever lived. Days later Jimmy Palmers was recycled into a newly unbreakable Ultimate Infinite Ink cartridge top of the range pen!

Elliot Rogers (10)
Morgans Primary School

A SNAKE DAY

5.00am
I start slithering through the Amazon Rainforest as quiet as possible. I look for food and when it is found, I wait and then . . . *snap*
'Mmmm.'

6.30am
When I see any danger I slither into the nearest hole. After the danger has passed I go back into the open and carry on searching.

8.00am
At last I've found a mouse . . . wait, steady on now.
'Mmm, big mouse.'
That feeds me for about three and a half hours.

9.30am
That mouse filled me up, so I will go and play
'Doowww . . . *goodness me* something just stung my rear end.'

11.00am
My rear end feels better now.
'Pooh, what's that smell?'
There was a skunk nearby, so I slithered as fast as my body could carry me.

12.30pm
Lunch time! I could smell some rats somewhere around me . . . yes, there they were five or six of them. Without another thought I snapped them up in one!

8.00pm
I've been searching for some dinner for half an hour. Now . . . hey, what's that, a tent. There has to be some humans in there, so I make a little hole and I gobble the human. Something then shot out my mouth. It said . . . 'Matthew Coks!'

Jack Stingemore (10)
Morgans Primary School

THE TALE OF THE RED BAT

Long (or not so long) ago, in a place far (or not so far) away, there lived a boy called Deaf Bat. He had a brother called Tomato Ketchup who he kept on a plate, under cling-film. One day, Tomato Ketchup pulled the cling-film aside, hopped onto the floor, went splosh, made a mess, and finally made his way into the garden.
'Hiya! Hedgey!' he said to his friend, Hedgey the hedgehog.
He liked stroking his hedgehog because the spikes went right through him.

Now, because Tomato Ketchup . . .
'Tomaty to you!' . . .
'OK, Tomaty.' Where was I? Yes! Now, because Tomaty was so small, he had many adventures. Here are some, as we step into Tomaty's boots . . .'

'Heeelllppp!' Tomaty moaned at the bacon who was laughing at the egg, who was squashed into the bread, who was stuffed in a bag, who was held by Slim Boy Fat.
'His breath smells!' I don't want to be in his stomach or intestine!'
'Mmmmm! Bacon! Egg! Bat! Bat? Yeuch!' said Slim Boy Fat, the dork in disguise.
'Ribbit!' It was the toad from next-door.
'Save me!' he cried, and he did! And *chomp! Gulp! Chomp! Gulp! Chomp! Gulp! Chomp!* His chomps and gulps drained away in the distance.
'Deaf Bat, it's time for tea! Mum is calling. See ya!'
Oh, before I go, that time he turned into The Red Bat was funny!'
'You evil witch, let me go!' I wailed, frantically trying to free myself. I was turned into a red bat! Only for a short while. Toad helped me again.

James Robinson (10)
Morgans Primary School

A DAY IN THE LIFE OF A DOG

Woof woof, ring ring, another day as a normal school girl. I got up wearily and went down to breakfast, Mum looked at me in amazement. She didn't know how I was walking on two legs and talking. For a moment I thought she had seen a ghost, but no it was true, I had four legs, a furry face and a big bushy wagging tail. I looked in the mirror. At first I thought I was dreaming, but no, it was true, I was a dog, a furry, smelly, flea-bitten dog. That moment I thought my life was over, but once I had thought about things I realised things wouldn't be so bad after all. I went back downstairs expecting toast and orange juice, but instead I got a bowl of dog food and a saucer of water. It wasn't very appetising, but I was so hungry I just ate it. I squeezed through the dog flap and set off.

I arrived at school. I went in with the caretaker and his trolley, went into the classroom and hid in Miss Grant's stock cupboard. The class came in at 8.50am. Ding, ding, ding, ding, finally it was break. I got off lucky today because we had a test. Miss Grant went to the staffroom and the pupils had left their tests on the desks for a moment. I had an urge to go and rip up the tests. I couldn't resist it, so I just chewed and chewed until I couldn't chew any more. I sauntered into the girls' toilets. I threw up everywhere. I felt awful, the worst I had felt in a long, long time. I walked slowly home. Once at home I lay on my bed. I had a funny feeling and two seconds later I was a girl. That was one of the best experiences ever.

Thayla Banks (10)
Morgans Primary School

A Day In The Life Of . . . Robbie Williams!

Press, press, press and even more *press!* Why can't they just leave me alone! First of all they make up stories like, I got married to Geri secretly, which is just not true and the next minute I'm having an affair with Nicole Appleton! I admit I am very close to Geri and I have been on several holidays, but we're just friends, it's nothing serious OK.

Can you believe I have two videos banned now, because I just happen to like being known as the Cheeky Boy in pop, it's not because I am trying to be rude or anything. Why can't people understand, oh well, Brit Awards soon.

Today I went to the Brit Awards - again, and Craig David got absolutely no awards and he is the best singer in R 'n' B. I wish I could've given him mine, ha ha, no chance. Hey did you see that really cool guy in the wet suit that looked like the inside of a human body, Emma Bunton looked like she could faint - I wish she had! Ha ha hee hee! Bono's face when Destiny's Child came on! He looked like he could walk right up there as he smiled so much! He said to me afterwards that Independent Woman is his favourite song by Destiny's Child and he had a chat with Beyonce after their performance. He is so lucky, but what I was looking forward to the most was when I took Geri Halliwell out to the London Met Bar after the awards, where we partied for a long time. Bryan from Westlife went a bit, how do you say, drunk! Me and Gezzy took him back to his London flat to recover and then we went home for the night full of strange dreams about drunken pop stars!

Jasmine Cowler (10)
Morgans Primary School

THE DAY AND LIFE OF MR JOLLY THE FISH

Hi, I am Mr Jolly and I am a large kind fish. I am going to tell you about the day and life of . . . well, me.

So let's begin. I live in a tank full of clean interesting equipment like shells, plastic plants, little stones to fill the bottom and rocks to play on.

I sadly have no play mates because my other three friends died. But luckily my owners are thinking about buying me a brand new tank-mate, so we can be friends and I won't be lonely.

Every morning my owners feed me flakes of fish food. It's so *yyuuummmmy* it's the best food in fish world.

I love to hide amongst the plants and stick my head inside a shell and when I see my owners coming, I swim to the top to be fed. Sometimes when they feed me I mistake their hands for food. I am very settled here in this kind and trusting home and it is really fun.

When my tank is empty and it needs cleaning my owners catch me in a net and put me in another bowl which is frustrating but good, because I get more food and some fresh air.

People say having a goldfish is a boring pet but my life is not even near the word boring because I decide what's boring and I say that a goldfish's life is *not boring!*

And that is the day and life about me.

Emily Wheeler (9)
Morgans Primary School

THE DAY IN THE LIFE OF POM POM

It was soggy and cold. I could not see anything but I could hear the squealing of other kittens. I squinted through my small eyes. I saw four other kittens huddled up together. I stumbled over to them and snuggled in.

I woke up in a cage by myself, no box, no wet stuff and no other kittens. Before I could start mewing a strong voice said 'I like this one, how much is she?'
I looked up and two people were pointing at me. A totally different voice said 'Well, this is the Cat's Protection League, so however much you want.'
I did understand what they said, but I didn't understand what they meant.

I was pulled out of the smelly cage and stuck in a basket. The basket was dim and it was carefully placed in the back of a huge blue thing, with four wheels. The blue thing started moving. I forced my way out of the basket to see what on earth was going on.

I hopped onto the back sill. There were things moving at about fifty miles an hour. Trees, grass, people, dogs, all going away from us. I stared for a couple of minutes then turned away.

Suddenly we braked. I went flying on to one of the people's laps in the front of the car. The person cuddled me, so I rolled over and went to sleep.

I woke up the next time they stopped outside a big, big house. They got out the car very sneakily, the woman took me and the man took the basket. We went inside into the studio. The people made a bed. It was only about four o'clock but I had had such a long day, I fell straight asleep. The next day I woke up in a wrapped up box, on a water bed.

I could hear voices of all kinds, a small girl and two much stronger voices. Then, light, the box opened, a small girl peered into the box, her small leaf green eyes stared for a few moments.

'She's so pretty,' she said, looking at me.

We bonded like we had been together in a previous life, maybe we had.

Emily Unwin (10)
Morgans Primary School

THE DAY AND LIFE OF KYM FROM HEAR'SAY

Hi, I'm Kym from Hear'say, the band. I'm going to tell you about the day and life of, well me, Kym.

As many of you would know I work in a band of five and they are called Myleene, Suzanne, Noel and Danny. I am going to tell you my life being a pop star on the very first day.

On that day I got chosen to be a pop star I thought that it was the happiest day of my life, but the thing that I got sad about was leaving my mum, dad and my brother. All of us didn't know who else was in the band, we were all really nervous about who is in the band with us. When we got to the house we saw all the others who were in the band. I liked and got used to every single one of them.

We got in the house, Nigel (the person who made us be pop stars) told us what we could and couldn't do. The house was all to ourselves! We found our rooms but Suzanne had to go into a room on her own at night.

We unpacked all of our bags. We had something to eat for tea. We watched TV for a while, then we went to bed. We talked a bit. Then we went to sleep!

That's my life being a pop star from Hear'say.

Danielle Leber (10)
Morgans Primary School

20TH AUGUST 1969

A golden beam of starlight seeped into the shuttle and made its way to a pair of sleepy eyes. The sleepy eyes slowly opened, to meet the magnificent gaze of space. Small pinpoint stars shimmered and sparkled, as the amazing shuttle turned to face the small satellite - known as the moon.

I raised my rested body and looked around. As my eyes focused, large computer screens were one of the first reassuring images to calm my very, very excited brain. I looked down at the ground, wait a minute! That's not right, I was floating in the air! Oh yea, I almost forgot, less gravity. I swept myself to the control room and sat in the lumpy chair. Next to a sturdy, tall figure, Buzz who in another lumpy chair had already started work. He grumbled something and then pushed a button. Michael too was already at work. Time seemed to fly as we prepared just like in the simulator.

The moment had come - separation, no turning back. Suddenly, the shuttle shook violently and then blasted forwards heading straight for the moon.

Fire! fire! Heat and rumbling erupted all at once. Thoughts ran through my head. Family, friends, teachers, but then suddenly, the shuttle stopped shaking and slowly touched the fragile surface of the moon.

I sat there stunned, realising for the first time that we had actually made it to the moon. In just a few hours, I, Neil Armstrong would step out onto the moon, knowing this is a small step for me, but one giant leap for mankind.

John Comer (10)
St Augustine's Catholic Primary School, Hoddeston

IN TIMES OF FIRE

He heard the clatter of the gun, the screaming of his enemies. The sound was immense; bursting through his ears. What was this? Rebels were entering! The attacker was shot with terribly brutal precision, his final words of evil content being 'game over'. -

'Turn that game off Michael,' screamed Mum.

Tom Newell (11)
St Columba's College and Prep School, St Albans

One Unfortunate Day

I had walked on paths though I had never set foot on it before. Combat was demanded. My abundance came up to me punching and kicking me as, I sprinted as fast as I could to reach base and home. But its safety had abandoned me.

'Turn that PlayStation off.'

Joseph Leadbetter (10)
St Columba's College and Prep School, St Albans

SURPRISE

I took my first step into the unexpected,
Beads of sweat rolled down my face,
I opened the door to the sitting room - the deserted sitting room,
I turned to go back, but I heard another noise,
I turned,
Then I had the fright of my life,
'Surprise!' my friends called loudly!

Jonathan Smith-Squire (11)
St Columba's College and Prep School, St Albans

GONE OVERBOARD

The enemies launched cannons at our ship,
several men went overboard and drowned
we fired back with our remaining gun
powder, cannons and man-power.
The deck filled with water, *'Ahh!'*
The captain yelled. Suddenly out of nowhere,
'Jack turn that game off!'
Mum yelled as Jack had gone overboard.

Francis Sales (11)
St Columba's College and Prep School, St Albans

SMOKY SPIN

Turning round the corner, accelerating down the start/finish line, smoke appears in my mirrors.

Into the first corner, the car spins into the grass and gravel.

I'm devastated.

A sign appears on my steering wheel, 'Game Over'

I turn off the game and hold my head low in dismay.

Blayne Pereira (11)
St Columba's College and Prep School, St Albans

CHORES

She'll kill me I know she will
All the threats.
I knew what would happen if I failed.
She will be here soon.

The door opened, then the footsteps,
in she came.
My fate was sealed.
'Nicholas, you haven't done the dishwasher
or set the table for dinner.'

Nicholas Kelliher (11)
St Columba's College and Prep School, St Albans

WORRYING

My first landing
Two hundred people's lives are in my hands
My hands are sweating
If I moved my feet I would lose concentration

I dare not speak at all
The last button pressed
I am so ready for the absolute worst
Success! With the landing on Flight Simulator 2000.

Adam Buckland (10)
St Columba's College and Prep School, St Albans

PREDATOR

I watch him. My eyes were riveted to him. His sharp, fierce claws dug
into the toy. His fur, golden, shining in the sunlight, his tail playing on
the ground. His green damp eyes were focused. I had to get out.
'Isn't he a cute little kitten,' said Mum, proudly.

Richard Purser (11)
St Columba's College and Prep School, St Albans

A DAY IN THE LIFE OF A PILOT

I woke up feeling excited and at the same time nervous. It was my first flight to France. I quickly got into my car and drove to the airport breaking the speed limit twice.

At the airport I handed my luggage in and went to the lounge to enjoy some coffee.
'Beep, can the pilot flying to France please board your plane.'
Shaking, I made my way up to the plane. When I got to the cockpit I started memorising all the buttons. The passengers started boarding. I remembered that I had to pretend to like them. I started my speech.
'Hello, I'm George Allcroft, your pilot and I hope you enjoy your journey.'
I pushed the throttle up and we were off. Starting to feel more confident I pointed the nose upwards and we left the floor. I swapped places with the co-pilot and sat back to enjoy the ride.

After a while it was time to land. After nagging the co-pilot to swap back I sat down in the pilot's chair and landed the plane. I dropped off to sleep in the plane for the next flight.

George Allcroft (10)
St Michael's CE Primary School, St Albans

A Day In The Life Of A Pilot In The World War II

Dear Eleanor and Mary,

I am writing to say I am still alive and uninjured. I hope you are well and your mother as well. I have not got my day of leave until next week so, I will love you until I die in this war, and if I live I will never stop loving you. Love from Your loving father Fred Metcalfe.

On 19th January 1940, I wrote to my daughter and wife to stop them worrying about me. I was in the war, I was in the RAF.

That day was when I crashed but struggled for my life. I was flying over the Pacific Ocean when my engine started to crackle. Before I knew it, the plane's nose was pointing down to the ocean. I was going to my death, I thought I would die, but then I remembered the small rubber boat inside the plane. I grabbed the boat and ejected my seat. As I landed heavily on the waves, the boat inflated quickly but had a hissing noise. All I could see was the ocean and all I could smell was salt water.

I searched for a battleship to take me home, but I could see nothing. The night went past slowly, in the morning I looked around for a ship and there south east from where I was floating, a ship coming closer rapidly.

I was going home.

Chloe Metcalfe (11)
St Michael's CE Primary School, St Albans

A DAY IN THE LIFE OF BART SIMPSON

I wake up to the sound of my sister's saxophone and turn to look at my Krusty The Clown clock. It says eight o'clock and the alarm goes off with a mighty 'Hey-hey!'
I get up, get dressed and jump out my window onto the tree. I then get my skateboard and head for the Kwik-e-mart.

I dodge Jimbo Jones and Nelson Muntz and get my order of a super syrup squishee and Radioactive man. Then I'm off to Moe's to collect my dad. By now it's one o'clock and I have to study for my history test tomorrow. I haven't even done a whole page of notes and I've had three hours.
Then I thought to myself, 'Time for some clownage,' and I turned on my bedroom television. Krusty the clown my hero, my idol on for four hours then another two of Itchy and Scratchy.
'This is the life, I thought to myself. But it wasn't for long . . .somehow my baby sister Maggie had got in my room and chewed on the cable. The television went black and the room became silent.

I decided to go and watch TV downstairs but I saw the Bartsignal, I crept outside and climbed up to my tree house and got on my Bartman gear. I went to Milhouse's house and worked out the mission. It was the Evil Canker aka Bob Teerwilleger. After a hard night's work I went home and went to bed and I said to myself,
'Aye Karumba, what a day!'

Edward Perchard (10)
St Michael's CE Primary School, St Albans

A DAY IN THE LIFE OF BART SIMPSON

Homer's alarm (which he puts on full volume) woke me up this morning. Mum called me for breakfast so I ran downstairs to my bowl of 'Krusty Flakes'.

'Bart, pass the milk please,' asked my sister, Lisa.
'No, I refuse!' I love annoying Lisa.
'Kids, come on, the school bus has arrived. Here are your lunches. Bart, hurry! Oh no, you've missed the bus.'
Marge (my mum) always hassles me. I ran to the garage, tucked my skateboard under my arm and knocked for my best friend, Milhouse.
'Hi Bart! Is Lisa here?'
'Milhouse I know you fancy Lisa, but can't you keep it quiet?'
I jumped on my skateboard and followed Milhouse.
'Ding-a-ling'.
Oh that's the bell. I shoved my skateboard in my locker and glanced at my watch. No wonder it's quiet - I'm late!
I hurried to the Principal's office, straightened up, knocked on the door and walked in.
'Sorry I'm late,' I mumbled.
Ten minutes later, I found myself struggling to stay awake in my worst lesson - maths!

'Ding-a-ling'. Cool man, that's the lunch bell. I gobbled down half of my lunch (gave the other half to Milhouse who forgot his). Before long, the bell went for the end of school. I grabbed my skateboard from my locker and raced Lisa home. I burst through our front door and leapt onto the couch and turned on the TV to Itchy and Scratchy.

Aaaah, this is the life!

Bryony Salmon (11)
St Michael's CE Primary School, St Albans

A DAY IN THE LIFE OF A PET HAMSTER

I woke up to the usual start - all of those strange, loud sounds of the morning. I had my daily morning exercise, I'm fed up of transport these days, you're either running in a wheel, without moving no matter how fast you run, or you're running around with this great big bubble around you! I heard my owner walking towards my cage, and suddenly the lid on the roof of my cage opened and the sunlight burst in. She called me but I couldn't understand her because she was speaking in human language. I hope that in a year I will have learnt at least two human words!

Soon everyone had left the house, Mmm! Peace at last! I climbed up my tunnel into the sleeping compartment to take my nap. I used to be completely nocturnal until I cam here because it's so loud in the mornings. I can't help staying awake!

Just as it was time for me to wake up, my owner had come home. I knew this because I was woken up by a tapping on the plastic of my cage. Oh well, it was time for me to wake up anyway. I climbed down my tunnel and she picked me up, she talked to me and expected me to understand her - I've got to start learning some human English!

Soon it was bedtime for her and escaping time for me. Now which plan should I use this time?

Hannah Crick (11)
St Michael's CE Primary School, St Albans

A Day In A Life Of Homer Simpson

Doughnuts . . . mmm!
'Homer, wake up, Homer!' Marge called.
'Doh, it was a dream!'
'Homer it's time to get up.
'Marge . . .!'

I got dressed into last week's clothes and headed for downstairs . . .
ahhh . . . crash!
'Bart!'
He left his skateboard at the top of the stairs, again.

Marge is putting me on a diet, that means no doughnuts, cake, beer, this is unfair! I walked into the kitchen for breakfast.

'Morning Homey,' she said like she does every morning. Marge walked out the room to have a shower. I quickly took Marge's toast and spread butter 4cm thick . . . mmm. I was still hungry so I reached to the top cupboards for doughnuts. I finished the five boxes that were piled up in the cupboard. I opened the fridge and took three beers, that were stacked at the back and went into the lounge to watch TV.

Five hours later . . .
'Homer are you watching TV and drinking beer?' Marge called.
'Er . . . no, I am sticking to my diet, I haven't eaten any doughnuts, or drunk any beer!'

One hour later . . .
'Here boy, here boy, go fetch beer!' the dog ran into the kitchen and grabbed a beer out of the fridge.
'Homer, why has the dog got a beer in his mouth?'
'Doh?'

Hannah Courtney (11)
St Michael's CE Primary School, St Albans

A DAY IN THE LIFE OF AN EVACUEE

3rd September 1939
Dear Dairy,
Today was the day I must go on the train to the country; Mother said I would probably be going to Norfolk to stay. (I hope the people in Norfolk will be kind.)

When Mother told me I was shocked, I was startled, I was absolutely terrified! I wouldn't have spoken to Mother for weeks but I wasn't stupid - I knew the seriousness of the situation. But still I couldn't stop the tears from brimming up in my eyes - how could she send me to live with someone I didn't even know? Still, at least I was getting evacuated with my little sister Peggy.

I wriggled into my school uniform, and squeezed into my leather shoes which were far too small for me..

As I buckled them nice and tight, I glanced over at Peggy who was fighting with her comb. Numbly I combed my own hair and fumbling helped Peggy into her own school uniform.

My legs felt like jelly as I stumbled towards the door I reached, and touched the door knob; but I couldn't do it. I couldn't leave my safe, safe home. I sat down with a sigh and a whimper, I sobbed into my hands for, I don't know how long.

The rest of the day was a blur - I was crying all the way through, I felt a bag being placed into my hand and a label being hung round my neck.

I never saw Mother again; maybe I'll find out some day.

Charlotte Phillips (11)
St Michael's CE Primary School, St Albans

A Day In The Life Of A Badger

'Mmmm, Hedgehog, Yummy!'

'Emily, Emily!'

'W-what's?' I gurgled through the dribble in my mouth, because I was enjoying my dream so much.

'Why did you wake me up from a delicious dream?' I snorted as my mum came into focus.

'You've missed breakfast. You need your lunch!'

I jumped into the air with these magical words, not because I'd missed breakfast, but lunch meant we were going hunting! I scrambled out of my muddy bed.

'Don't forget to wash, darling!'

Once I had replied, I started washing myself. I put my tongue on my paws and started licking.

Once I was completely clean, I led my family out into the wilderness. Rustle, rustle.

'Hedgehog!' I whispered, I pounced!

I dragged the dying hedgehog out.

Oliver came over and asked why we had to kill it and I told him that we needed to eat them to survive. For the first time in my life I felt a centimetre of sorrow. But it went away when my senses picked up an earthworm. I started digging. Then I let my little brother find the worm.

'I'll give you a race,' questioned my sister.

Oliver and I both told her that we would love to. My mum and dad dragged the hedgehogs and the worms, because they had also found some animals.

When we got home, we all ate.

'Mmm!' we kept saying as our jaws plunged into the food. We all got into bed, because we'd had such a exhausting day.

Emily Attwood (11)
St Michael's CE Primary School, St Albans

A Day In The Life Of Red Rum

I pawed the ground, with anticipation, on my wood shavings, in the finest stables on the racecourse.

My groom came in because my owner was ill.

'Hello Rum! How are you eh?' he said gruffly.
Ben - also one of the finest grooms - put a loose fitting blanket on with a leather head collar with gold buckles. He led me out and walked me around to get used to the course.

Oooh it feels sooo good to stretch my big powerful muscles!

I walked past the 'weighing in room' and the 'jockey's bar' to get to the course itself. I pulled on the lead rope, anxious to run, free, galloping, stretching my legs!

Later on in the day my jockey came and you will not believe how many people came. There was a hub bub of excitement and a commentator was blasting into the microphone. My groom came in again and put on my light weight saddle and bridle. I looked stunning.

In the starting box, I waited as a horse reared at going into it and was being blind folded. They opened and I was off!

'Number seven, Red Rum in second place . . .' the commentator shouted.

I reached out, running free with my jockey, overtaking chestnut blurs. I was in first place!
'Run run run . . .' my jockey was chanting. 'Go go!'
'Red Rum came in first!' they all shouted.

Emily Moxom (11)
St Michael's CE Primary School, St Albans

A DAY IN THE LIFE OF MY RABBIT DIZZY

I scramble out of the hay box after a long sleepless night. Great, I've eaten all of my food, so now I have to wait for Rosie to come and feed me.

At last she's coming out. My food, crunch, crunch, munch, munch, yum. My eyes are distracted by the fact that I have new cold water slurp, slurp.

My life is really boring but I can do some cool tricks eg I can flip a cup over my head. I have to wait ages before Rosie comes back to play with me. I get very bored because during the day I don't have company (I wish I had a friend.) I eat, drink and sleep during the day. I really miss Rosie. Oh no it's Puzzle the cat - sometimes I think that she is going to eat me.

Six hours later Rosie comes back from school and comes out to see me. She gives me grass. She says she misses me at school and she loves me. Whilst she goes to the park Emily (Rosie's sister) has to play with me and she's rather boring. She's too loud so I don't really like her.

My day ends at 8.30pm when Rosie gives me more dried food and covers my run with a blue cloth to stop cats and foxes from injuring me. I try to get to sleep but I'm too lonely and scared to sleep.

Rosie Wills (11)
St Michael's CE Primary School, St Albans

A DAY IN THE LIFE OF JAMES BOND

Da Dada Da! Hi I'm James Bond, now let me tell you a story. It all happened when I was getting ready to serve M in a war against Renard and his men. I was quite surprised to see him still alive. He had a bullet in his head. He will die but he'll grow stronger every day until he does. While I was getting ready I was feeling a bit dodgy but was going to fight him. I needed to drive to where I knew he was hiding out.

Bbbrrrmmm! Man I love this BMW, missiles, guns, bullet proof, etc . . . millions of stuff. I was frozen 'cause I was so scared that I might lose the battle against Renard but still I carried on. As soon as I got there I bashed the door of the secret warehouse down, he and his men were covered in sawdust and dust from where I'd bashed the door down. Renard stood forward and drew his gun slowly at the same time that I did. We both shot one at a time like two cowboys in battle, but we kept on missing. Finally I shot him in the heart and he fell dead on the floor.

While I was driving home to my wife Electra and my thirteen year old son, I was thinking that in the future he will be my student and will do all the training and fighting that I have done all these years. It is dangerous but I just know he will love the adventure!

Samuel Townsend (10)
St Michael's CE Primary School, St Albans

A DAY IN THE LIFE OF LOIS (MY CAT)

I woke up and clambered out of my bed. I still felt sleepy so I decided to go outside for some fresh air. It was dark but not cold.

The 'Uprights' won't be downstairs until seven o'clock and so I think I'll go and adventure next-door. Felix says mice are swarming everywhere. I'll bring one home for the 'Uprights' as a present.

I prowl along the road and jump onto the wall, balancing perfectly before flying down onto the dew covered grass. Placing my wet paws carefully so not to give my presence away to the mice. Something darts from one patch of leaves to another. I build up strength ready to pounce then lean forward, lift my head and the wind blows . . .

I glide forward, paws outstretched the mouse scurries across the lawn and I fall flat on my whiskers and stand up as if nothing ever happened. Every time it happens the pain isn't as bad I scanned the grass. I'd had enough for now but I'd be back later.

Once I was home I waited for my breakfast all that energy makes you starving. One of the 'Uprights' suddenly burst through the kitchen door. She's called Kate.

'Lo lo pussy breakfast,' she said picking me up and stroking me.
I gobbled down my food and went to find a nice comfy sofa or bed. I found Edward's. I huddled in the covers and fell asleep.

Kate Lindeman (11)
St Michael's CE Primary School, St Albans

A Day In The Life Of My French Au Pair (When I Was Six)

Bonjour, I am called Celine and I am an au pair for an English girl called Sophie. She is six. J'aime Sophie, sorry, in English um, er, I *like* Sophie. She is good to me and helps me to learn English.

Anyway, back to my day. I took Sophie to school. This is unusual for me, as it is a Wednesday. In France, she wouldn't be going to school; she would be having a wonderful day going swimming in the sun and sunbathing (as it is June) and . . . snap out of this daydream of the sun: it's cold here.

So, I left Sophie at school and walked into town where there are some nice shops. Then I went back to the house to have some lunch, fromage on toast (translation: cheese on toast).

Tonight I will go out with my friends. We will try not to stay out too late. We will go to the cinema. I hope I will understand the film, although I might not. But it should be good being with my friends anyway.

Now I am going to write my diary . . .

'Dear Diary

aujourd'hui, j'ecris mon journal en Anglais! (Today, I am writing my diary in English!) Today is cold, but it's a good day anyway because I am going out with my friends later . . . I must go now, it's 3.15pm and I have to collect Sophie . . .'

I have collected Sophie. Later . . . Anita, Sophie's mum is back and I'm off to *party!*

Sophie Hemery (10)
St Michael's CE Primary School, St Albans

How The War Broke Out

One day at 7.30am everyone was asleep apart from my grandad. He was just getting his breakfast when he over-heard two men talking about a war going to break out, but then he realised that the two men were the enemies. At the time my grandad hurried to tell someone, luckily his friend across the road.

Lunch time 12.00pm my grandad had found the police station and now the police were showing the scene on TV. Earlier in the afternoon people were watching the birds with their telescopes and they saw the enemy were near, so the war broke out and all the children and grownups had to get a job. My grandad was helping with the planes.

Teatime 9.00pm he was invaded by the enemy and my grandad had a very little finger because he had his little finger chopped off and now when I go to his house I always say 'Can I look at your little finger?'
He always tells us one of his stories and some of the stories are really gross and we say 'Er that is gross' and we have a lovely time and we don't want to go home. We have to go home and when we go home we tell Mum about it and Mum makes us go to sleep.

Sarah Webb (9)
Stanley Junior School

A DAY IN THE LIFE WITH HANNAH

7am in the morning, Hannah got up, got dressed and went to meet her other friends in S Club 7. She and her friends went to the gym and started dancing to practise for a show.

'Come on guys, let's get going, it's our show today,' said Paul. They stayed at the gym for four hours and still had two hours to go. Two hours later Hannah went back home for a rest and a cup of tea and breakfast. When she got up later she had to go to the park and meet the rest of S Club 7. All the girls were going around looking at clothes to wear at the show.

'Hey Hannah,' said Jo, 'here's some nice clothes, let's go and have a look inside and get them. So they did.
'Come on, we've only two hours left,' said Hannah. They were on their way when they saw the boys. They all walked to where they were going to do their show. They put their clothes on and started practising.
'Don't stop moving . . .' sang Hannah. They all practised at least 40 times.

'Come on guys, I'm worn out let's sit down,' said Paul.
'Hey guys,' said the man who was filming, 'one hour till the show starts.'

An hour later, the show started.

'Ladies and Gentlemen,' said Mike, 'welcome to S Club 7.'

'Don't stop moving . . .' sang Hannah.

Two hours later, everybody was tired out.

'I'm going home,'

'Me too.'

'Me too.'

'And me.'

'And me.'

'And me too.'

'Don't forget about me.'

When Hannah got home, she had a shower and a cup of tea and a biscuit then went to bed. In the morning there was to be another show.

'Oh no, I'll have to do the same thing all over again,' said Hannah.

Alicia Davies (9)
Stanley Junior School

A DAY IN THE LIFE OF CAPTAIN HARDY

I am going to write about what Captain Hardy did in his day. He was a captain of a great battleship called HMS Victory. He was in charge of all the crew but Admiral Horatio Nelson was in charge of him, all the ship and the crew.

One day, Captain Hardy was lying in bed asleep, it was 4am. He was dreaming about a sea battle that they had won the other day. By the time he had stopped dreaming, it was seven o'clock. It was time to get up so he took off his night-cap and pyjamas and put on his big, black hat, his navy blue coat and his white trousers. Then he put on his shoes and went to wake the crew. At half-past seven he and the crew waited on the deck of the ship for the Admiral to greet them. The cabin door opened and Admiral Nelson let them into his cabin for breakfast.

After breakfast the Captain ordered the crew to set sail. So the crew raised the anchor and HMS Victory set sail. After a few hours at sea, it was time for lunch. Captain Hardy listened to Nelson's plans while eating his lunch. But then, many hours later, a pirate ship was seen on the horizon. It was coming towards them. Captain Hardy grabbed the ship's wheel and Nelson watched the crew turn the sails and they tried to outrun the pirates. But the pirate ship was catching up and soon the two ships were side by side. All the weapons were drawn. Then all the pirates jumped aboard the Victory. A great battle began!

Nelson and his captain fought the leaders of the pirates. Smoke filled the air as swords clashed and clashed everywhere.

A few hours passed and the pirates were losing. All the leaders were dead and there were only a few pirates left alive. The pirate chief knew he would lose but he thought he could escape the ship alive. But first he wanted to blow up the ship!

Captain Hardy saw him lurking around. He followed him to the hold which was the bottom deck. Just as he was about to light a bomb, Hardy leapt out from his hiding place and charged at the chief. The chief spun around and raised his sword. They battled back and forth. Suddenly, Captain Hardy leapt to one side of the chief and swung his sword so hard that he fell over backwards. He quickly leapt to his feet but the chief pirate wasn't there! He was lying on the floor, eyes closed. The huge swing with his sword must have killed him.

'May your afterlife forgive you,' said Captain Hardy.

That night Nelson gave Hardy a medal for his bravery. After Nelson had left his cabin, Hardy climbed into bed. 'All's well that ends well,' Hardy whispered to himself. Then he fell asleep.

James Mearman (9)
Stanley Junior School

A DAY IN THE LIFE OF ALLISON

6 o'clock in the morning. I get up to go to the loo. I am going to play
the part of Willow from Buffy
'Wa, wa!' Hang on, that is my son, Jim.
My name is Allison, OK. That's better, all quiet.
'Wa wa!' Maybe not, I have to go to work now so (slam).

'Allison, come on, you are on. We want you to play the part of Willow
doing a spell.'
'OK' said Sarah. Sarah plays the part of Buffy.
('Scent-sations') I said.
Brrnng! That is the lunch bell. Yum, yum, I have got bacon, lettuce and
tomato sandwiches. Yum, that was scrummy.
Brrnng! That's the end of lunch.
'Sarah, can you play the part of Killing Angel.'
David plays the part of Angel.
Coffee break. I don't like the coffee here so I'm having apple juice. 55
minutes more till the end of work.
'David, are you watching ER tonight?'
'Yes.'
Brrnng! 'End of coffee break. I better be getting back now.'
'No, you won't, not without finishing your job, just do one more spell
for us, OK?'
('Scent-sations') I said. 'Now can I go home?'
'Yes, thank you.'
Oh, oh, a traffic jam, but it is only on the news. I forgot to shut the door
(slam!). I'm so tired I am going to bed, no, it is only 9 o'clock. I will go
at 10 o'clock.
'Wa wa!' It is Jim again. I will go and put him to bed and I will go to ,
'Hor chue!' that's him and this is me, 'Hor chue.'
I am not really asleep but now I am.

zzzzzzzz!

Willow Malin (9)
Stanley Junior School

A Day In The Life Of Britney On Tour

Dear Diary,
Today I did rehearsals. OK, how about yesterday? Let me think.
I know, on tour . . .

5.25 in the morning, time to wake up even though I didn't get any sleep anyway. People banging at the door and these beds are so uncomfortable.
Half an hour later, 'OK I'm here.'
'Britney, you're late again, now get to rehearsal.'
Rehearsals for tonight take ages, stop, start again, stop, start again, where can you ever get a break around here?
Even worse was the autograph signing, firstly, I couldn't get through the crowd and secondly there were five ambulances. At least one thing went right, the concert! Wow! That was great! People screaming and cheering me on.
I've never done such a great concert.
It was sad when I had to leave, I had a great time.
I phoned my mum to tell her I was coming home. I waved goodbye and got on the plane. I was so happy to see my mum and family. I gave them all huge hugs and we had a big meal for my homecoming.
'Britney, your boyfriend's at the door.'
'OK Mum.'
Well, I've got to go now, bye!
'Let's go for a movie!'
'Great!'

Emily Hatton-Smith (9)
Stanley Junior School

A DAY IN THE LIFE OF MY DAD

Beep, beep, beep, beep! That's all my dad hears in the morning. The alarm is set for 6.15 but my mum gets up at 6.30 so my dad makes her breakfast in bed. Then he sips his coffee and relaxes while my mum struggles to get into the bathroom to get ready for her school.

After he has got washed and dressed, he gets me and my brother, Mitchell, ready for school and then takes us to school. After he has dropped us off, he hobbles (for he has had an operation on his foot) back home.

He then does the chores my mum has told him to do. He does the ironing, hoovering, washing up, tidying up and mends some of my mum's school toys. After he has done these jobs, he relaxes in front of the television and watches motorcycling. After Valentino Rossi has pulled off another win, he pops off to Sainsbury's to get food for the family.
'£10.00!' exclaims my dad sarcastically at the price of beers. After he has done the shopping he picks us up from school and we tell him what we have learnt.

When he goes into the playroom he sees the mess and booms 'Boys!' and gets us to tidy it up. When Mum comes home, he makes us a lovely lasagne and we gobble it up. Then after we (and my dad) watch Dragonball Z we go and practise football until it's time for a bath. When we're in bed, he creeps down and fixes all our broken toys.

What a wicked dad, even if he has had an operation on his foot!

Murray Maynard (9)
Stanley Junior School

A Day In The Life Of Mrs Nickolson

One day Mrs Nickolson woke up in her bed with lots of cats on the cover. She got out of bed and strolled into the bathroom, washed her face with soap and water and then brushed her teeth with an electric toothbrush. The bathroom was blue with a white sink, bath, and a white-framed mirror.

After that she walked into the bedroom and got dressed in a dress with flowers on it and a cardigan. Once she had put her make-up on she walked down the winding staircase and went into the kitchen, poured out a bowl of cornflakes and ate them all up.

At 8.30 she set off for school. Mrs Nickolson was a teacher at Stanley Junior School in Year 4. Anyway, as I was saying, she drove to school, went into the playground and got 4J, her class.

'Today we are going to make Greek pots,' she said.
So we put flour on the tables and she handed out clay.
'Shape the clay into pots, use a lot of water.'
12.15 'Lunchtime. Tables A, B and C, go out and get your lunch, then Table D.'
Mrs Nickolson went to the staffroom to eat her lunch.
13.15. Mrs Nickolson got her class to finish their pots.
15.20. 'Home time.'
Mrs Nickolson went home to make supper and put a bowl of cat food out for the cats and went to bed.

Talulah Gaunt (9)
Stanley Junior School

A DAY IN THE LIFE OF MY DAD

My dad gets out of bed at 7.00 and is extremely tired because he was woken up in the middle of the night by my little brother. Anyway he gets dressed and as soon as he has finished, he wakes us up in a loud voice and uses an even more waking-up-type voice when my brother and I don't wake up. When we are finally woken up and dressed, my dad asks us what kind of cereal we want. We all go down for breakfast. My dad has his breakfast and then he gets his coat, shoes, helmet and rucksack with a load of things, too many inside it, and runs down the garden to get on his bike, forgetting to do his shoelaces up and trips, ties up his shoelaces and climbs on his bike. He cycles quickly to work because he is very late.

When he gets to work he has to do some boring marking because he works as a teacher in College. These are the things he does after that: he searches the web on the computer but the computer crashes, he meets up with one of the students, the student borrows Dad's calculator and Dad has to mark maths for half an hour without a calculator.

By the time Dad gets home he is really tired, so straight after tea he decides to go to bed.

Luke Askwith (9)
Stanley Junior School

A Day In The Life of Curiosity And Harry

There was once a kitten called Curiosity who was very curious. She always had fun adventures but today was better than ever.

Curiosity ran away from home one day and found an old woman waiting for a bus. 'Come on, when is the bus going to get here?' said the woman not knowing that Curiosity was behind her. Just then Curiosity slipped into the woman's bag and went onto the bus with the old woman.

Inside the bag Curiosity was putting on some of the woman's lipstick, it was bright red. Curiosity liked it. 'Um,' thought Curiosity, 'I will get out of here and have an adventure.' So Curiosity slipped out of the bag and went outside.

Back inside the kitten's home, Curiosity's owner was looking all over for her. 'Curiosity, where are you?' but Samantha, her owner, could not find her anywhere.

Curiosity was walking along a jungle. She saw a lion fighting there. Well, it looked like a lion to Curiosity. Suddenly Curiosity fell down a very deep hole, it was very wide and long, it looked like it would never end. Just then Curiosity hit the ground and saw Geri Halliwell singing her new song 'It's Raining Men'. Curiosity loved that song and went up to her while she was dancing in the jungle.

'Ruff, ruff, ruff,' said Harry, Geri's dog. Curiosity remembered that she was still wearing the lipstick and Harry fancied her with it on. Geri was on her lunch break and saw Harry and Curiosity with each other. Curiosity saw Robbie Williams with Geri. 'Come on Geri, let's have some lunch,' said Robbie admiringly and Curiosity and Harry got married.

Jodie Harn (9)
Stanley Junior School

A Day In The Life Of Streak, The Blackbird

I am preparing to fly to Australia, and I am feeling excited as it is my first flight alone. I have taken off, and I am already halfway there. I see trouble up ahead. It is a hurricane! I desperately try to turn around, but it is already upon me. I am being battered and bruised by the winds, which must be force nine . . .

For the next three hours I struggled to stay alive, until my head cracked against something. It was a ship's mast. I hung onto that ship's mast for all I was worth for I knew that letting go meant certain death. I slowly crawled down the mast literally in centimetres. I got inside the cabin and saw, for the first time, the owner of the boat. He was a kind fellow and bandaged my head for me. I spent the next 11 hours with him until the boat crunched on a sandy beach. I learnt later that it was Bucklands Beach, the main harbour around Howick, Auckland. I was by this time better and flew to make myself a nest. I was in New Zealand, Aotearoa. I quickly selected a pohutikawa tree, as its red, rosy flowers and leaves provided shelter for me. I had already decided that from that day on, I would never fly across the sea again. Except, perhaps, in an aeroplane.

Tom Alpe (10)
Stanley Junior School

DRACULA, THE BLOOD-SUCKING VAMPIRE BAT

I woke up feeling mean and selfish. I fluttered to get up and felt hungry, flying out of my cave. I spotted a great big fat rat, I swooped down and sucked its blood out in one gulp. It was a lovely night so I decided to make the most of it.

I flew around for a bit. I didn't have any friends, I didn't want any. I had another rat and seven more mice that night until I started to feel tired so I went back to my cave.

The next night I woke up and flew out. I was hungry, there was a frog, quick, oh, this is nice.
'Hi, can you be my friend?' said a voice.
I looked round and saw another bat.
'No, go away,' I snarled, 'I don't have friends.'
'Why not? Friends are the nicest things in the world,' the bat exclaimed.
'So I'm not nice, am I?'
'I don't know. I don't know you, what's your name?'
I thought about it.
'Dracula,' I said.
'Well, can you be my friend?'
'No, I'm nice, I don't have friends, now go away,' I shouted.

I couldn't sleep last day, that little bat had been getting on my nerves, he thinks I'm lonely. Anyway, he's quite fun.
'Getting up or not?' I heard him shout.
'Coming,' I yelled.
'You are really nice,' he said as I came to meet him.

It sounds like life is going to be a lot . . .
'Hurry up,'
        . . . Harder!

Rachel Parker (9)
Stanley Junior School

A Day In The Life Of Jamie Oliver!

I woke with a start to a beautiful morning. I had just thought of a pukka recipe, a spicy tomato sauce. Oh, my last tomatoes were in last night's salad. So off I went to Sainsbury's on my motorcycle (and I got all my ingredients). Leaving the doors of Sainsbury's there was a massive crowd of people asking for my autograph. Suddenly I remembered my friends were coming for lunch! A reward for helping with the decorating.

When I got back they were waiting outside my door.
'Jamie, where have you been, mate?'
'Sorry I needed to get some food from Sainsbury's.'

The tomato sauce was great with pasta and it worked well with a special salad I had made the night before.

When we had finished, we got a video from Apollo, 'Charlie's Angels', the video was really good and my friend fell head over heels for Cameron Diaz, who he really likes. It was eight o'clock and we decided to play a game of charades . . . it was my go and I was Drew Barrymore. My friend got it in one and I mean, *one* go! (I think the silhouette gave it away.) He decided to be Brad Pitt which took us forever to get.

'Jamie, I need to go home, the baby-sitter will cost a fortune.'
'Yeah mate, I need to go as well, I'm going out really early tomorrow.'
'OK, bye. See you on Tuesday.'
'Bye Jamie, see ya.'

Milly Alim (10)
Stanley Junior School

A Day In The Life Of Kym From Hear'say

I wake up feeling really nervous and really sick and anxious to find out whether I am in the band. I wonder who else is? My mum and dad are comforting me. Suddenly, there's a knock at the door.

I nearly faint as I open the door and see Paul, one of the judges, looking freezing cold. I let him in to meet my parents then I show him to the living room, that's when the tension starts. There's silence then . . .

'You're in,' he says.
'Aaaahhh!' I scream, *'Oh my God!'*

I run into the kitchen where my mum and dad are. They had kind of guessed I was in as I was happy and hugging them. All I wonder now, is who else is in the band?

I'm in the car; I meet Suzanne, there's hugging and 'well dones' and everything. Then we get to the house. Wow, it's huge! Myleene, Danny and Noel are there, the whole band together, wow, I'm so happy!

After lots of tiring rehearsals we enter the charts with 'Pure and Simple', our only competition to stop us getting number one is Westlife.

We're number 1!

But if only I could be the number 1 Mum.

Sarah Hollinshead (10)
Stanley Junior School

A DAY IN THE LIFE OF JACQUELINE WILSON

Feeling refreshed from her brisk fifty lengths, she ate her muesli with chopped bananas. While she did this, she pondered upon her coming book. The thing that puzzled her was the title, it had to be witty but not silly.

She sat down with a pad to write ideas for the title. The book was about twins, whose mum died and their dad had found a partner whom they didn't like, so it had to be about twins. Jacqueline thought for a bit then it struck her 'Double Play! No, Double Act!' she screamed.

As a break, she thought she would phone her daughter. The next thing she knew she was having a long conversation. As she ended the call, some post arrived. Jacqueline was so excited 'cause there might be a letter of acceptance for Double Act! But it was just a letter from her penfriend Katie! She opened the next one but it was just the mortgage bill.

By now it was 5 o'clock, time to go to the Smarties Awards to collect her book, 'Glumbslime'. She waited and waited ages but she didn't win an award!

At nine, she drove home, tired and ready for bed. She had eaten her dinner at the ceremony. Exhausted she crawled up the stairs and into her pyjamas, and struggled into bed with a six-inch book. Soon she was fast asleep.

Caitlin Dorgan (10)
Stanley Junior School

A DAY IN THE LIFE OF A ROCK

I am a little rock, I have a very good life because all I do all day is lie on the beach feeling the cold water getting washed up on me. In the afternoon I got picked up by a little girl, her hands were very hot and very slippy. I was very lucky because I got to go in a box with other rocks like me.

I got picked up again from the box, the girl put me in her pocket and went to her friend's house but I fell out on the road, and got run over by a car. It was very painful. I was lucky because I got picked up by a little boy and he took me home and washed me with some water and cleaned me so much that I was nice and shiny again. He put me on his bedside table and gave me a name, the name was Toby. I liked that name. He was going to go down to the supermarket with his mum. He didn't drop me so that was very good but he dropped me on the way home. I found another home in a rock collector's box. He polished me with some extra special rock polisher he had made. I was very happy with my new home with my rock collector and my rock friends in the box.

Chantelle Josefsohn (9)
Stanley Junior School

A DAY IN THE LIFE OF ZOLA

At 6.00 Zola gets out of bed and gets dressed, and goes downstairs. He has breakfast then feeds his kids. Then about 7.30 he says goodbye. He's off to work at Stamford Bridge. He puts his football kit in the changing rooms and says hello to the players. Zola is a striker for Chelsea. Now he's one of the best players. Zola warms up for half an hour then after that he trains for about two hours. The best bit is playing each other.

'Zola, I was meant to tell you about this, tomorrow morning, we're playing Man U at their stadium. Who do you think's going to win, Zola?' said Jimmy.

Zola said, 'Definitely Chelsea. What time does it start?'

'1.00 to 2.30.'

'We're the best team ever, we want so badly to win,' said Zola.

When lunchtime came, Zola and Jimmy said, 'Let's have a burger for lunch.'

After lunch Zola said, 'Bye, see you tomorrow at the match.' He went home, knocked on the door and his girlfriend opened the door. He said to her, 'I'm playing Man U tomorrow.'

'Dad, are you playing tomorrow?' said his son.

'Yes, I am playing.'

'Who against?' said his son.

'Man U.'

'Dad, you can beat them,' said his son.

'Course he can,' said Zola's girlfriend.

'I'm going to bed,' said Zola.

'So am I,' said his son.

Cameron Serridge (9)
Stanley Junior School

A Day In The Life Of A Book

Hi, I'm a book. Yesterday I was in a shop, now I'm here, terribly cold and I don't like the way my new owner treats me.

She's just stopped reading me, and I'll tell you how she marks her place. She folds back the top corner of the page and closes me. Oh no, she's come into the room, she might want to read me.

Hello, I'm back again, she completely finished reading me and I'm in her car with lots of other books. We're now in a strange place. I mean me and all the other books. Oh no, I think we're at a car boot sale.

I'm on a strange table with loads more books I haven't seen before. The car boot sale is open now and there are people everywhere.

There is a man at the table buying me. I'm now in his pocket with a lot of other things, string, a watch, gloves and a wallet.

Well, bye for now, see you again on another small adventure.

Katherine Williamson (9)
Stanley Junior School

A Day In The Life Of A £2 Coin

It was a rainy day and a £2 coin was on the floor. Just then a boy came along and picked it up and went into the shop to buy some sweets but they were five pounds. He did have five pounds but as he picked it out of his pocket, the £2 coin was on the top of the £5 note. As he was paying, it rolled off. It rolled out of the shop. The boy went running after it but a man picked it up and chucked it down the drain.

The next day he was walking down by the river and he saw the coin right in the middle of the river and five minutes later a boat came along and knocked the coin towards the edge. He picked it out of the water and went home.

Christopher Sheldrake (9)
Stanley Junior School

A Day In The Life Of An Army Commander

I am an army commander, the date is 1939. It is the Second World War. Our mission is to take over and destroy the German air base. I have fifty men with grenades, mines and Uzis.

'Attack.'

That was Squadron One attacking the enemy turrets.

'Captain.'

'Yes soldier.'

'Enemy turrets are destroyed. You and your men can go in now.'

I run to the door, open it and throw grenades at five men. They die a second later. I call in my men. Two big machine guns shoot from nowhere and kill twenty men. We run for cover behind the two big columns in the hallway.

Two of our snipers destroy the droid guns and send in ten men with Uzis (machine guns). They make it all the way to the machine gun turrets. Five of them are shot, the rest destroy the turrets. At last they make it to the main hangar, which is enormous, and shoot the pilots. I run in and am shot in the leg. My men shoot all the enemies. We plant mines on all the planes and a bomb in the generator and run out and blow it up. Just then two planes destroy all my men with missiles. I take my rocket launcher and shoot them down.

Alasdair Fraser (9)
Stanley Junior School

A Day In The Life Of A Falcon

I am a falcon. I have a fan like tail and short wings. I have white fluffy plumage around my eyes. I have sharp, needle like, elegant talons. My beak is curved and razor sharp. I am a bird of prey. At the moment I am flying over the Mediterranean at 127 miles per hour. I have reached land and I'm having a small snack.

'This is better than the ones in England. It's a gerbil, by the way.'

I must move on now if I want to get to the mating ground. I am nearly there, it will take one more hour. There are some hunters shooting at me.

'Oh no.'

Bang, bang.

'Phew,'

Bang

'That was close.'

I'm in the mating ground now but I'm going right to the centre of the nesting ground. There are tigers and elephants below me. There's a mouse in my nest. I'll eat it quickly. Now I'll attract a mate.

'Look, a flock of eagles . . . '

'Run for it.'

'We are flying away now.'

'Bye.'

Patrick Davis (9)
Stanley Junior School

A Day In The Life Of A Purse

I am a purse and I am going to tell you about the day I was bought.

It was Saturday and I was the only teddy bear purse left in the shop. I was very happy there because I had all my friends with me. You may think I am mad but I didn't actually want anyone to buy me!

But the day always comes when you're bought. Yes, just a few hours after the shop had opened, I was taken off the shelf and put on the counter for a little girl called Lucy. She asked how much I was. I knew how much I was.
'One pound ninety-nine,' said the lady.
But thankfully the girl only had one pound. She was just about to put me back when the lady said,
'Do you really want it?
'Well, yes I do,' said Lucy.
'Come on then, have it for one pound.'
So the girl (Lucy) took me out of the shop and went home.

When we got home, she put me on the staircase. A few hours later her mother called her for supper. On the way, Lucy picked me up and put me in her bedroom drawer.

I'm still in here and she takes me out when she goes shopping. Even better, she takes me to my shop!

Molly Avigdor (9)
Stanley Junior School

A Day In The Life Of A Fork

One day a fork was sitting on the table ready for breakfast in the house of the Wests. They were very kind people.

The children came racing downstairs for breakfast. The youngest picked up the fork and started to stab bacon with it.

'Hi, I am the fork, it's . . . I suppose . . . OK being a fork, apart from the fact that you are always, well nearly always dirty. Anyway I am just about to be put in someone's mouth and I don't like this bit. When you are really dirty, they put you in this thing called a . . . urr . . .umm . . thingybob. Well never mind what it's called because I don't know anyway. And then you get put in a boxy thing and they put powder in the box and shut it up. Then hot water falls on you and you get really hot and sweaty. Then they take you out and put you in a drawer and you sit there all night and get hot. Then they take you out again and the whole thing starts all over again.'

See I told you, It was a boring life.

Kate Facer (9)
Stanley Junior School

A Day In The Life Of A Soldier

I am a soldier. I am in the navy. Yesterday I had a battle. My machine gun killed 400 men. My bazooka killed 500 men. When all was lost we fled into the forest where we had to cross a minefield, so I decided to use the minesweeper. Just then suddenly a great metal machine gun bullet plunged into my leg, it was as painful as being run over by a tank. My recruits tried to help me, but on the way they were very painfully hit by hundreds of spine breaking bullets. I grabbed my favourite and best recruit while I was still on the ground, and I grabbed his machine gun. While still crawling on the ground with my recruit, I shot ten more men. Then I noticed in the distance an enemy tank approaching so I quickly jumped onto the back and strapped my recruit to the tank with my belt. I opened the hatch to the inside of the tank and crazily shot both of the enemies in there. and threw the men out of the tank and onto the ground. I brought the recruit inside. I knew we were far from base camp but I knew where it was. After a tiring four hours, we got to base camp again and, two hours later the bullets were out of me and my recruit and we were both up and running again.

Alex Melehy (9)
Stanley Junior School

THE ORIGIN OF HYPERSONIC!

7am

'I am Supersonic! I am the lesser known double of Sonic the Hedgehog. Today I put off my quest to destroy Sonic and have decided to destroy Planet Earth! First I'll destroy parliament and I warn you, I am invincible!' roared Supersonic as he walked through London.
'Fazakah! Fifteen tanks down, eighteen to go! The earthlings are weak!' thought Supersonic, 'although a single being can stop me!'

10am

'Parliament is spared! The one person who can stop me is . . . Captain Chaos! Send him to me! Then only half of your population will be destroyed!'
Now the whole world was in trouble. Captain Chaos was chasing the stars! But Professor Bingbong Shondon had the answer. *Hypersonic,* a clone of Supersonic! He could defeat Supersonic!

1pm

'Where are you?' said Hypersonic.
Fazakah!
'I'm here!' shouted Supersonic.
'You feeling lucky, punk?' said Hypersonic, 'man or mouse?'
'I'll find out!' exploded Supersonic.

Fazzakah! Kaboom! Shazzaskom! Fazzakah! Kaboom! Shassaskom!

Supersonic lay low, defeated! Slowly he sailed away!

The end . . . or is it? *Ha, ha, ha!*

William Webb (9)
Stanley Junior School

BILL AND TED'S AMAZING ADVENTURE

Bill and Ted wanted to be rock stars but the words didn't fit in. So Bill had an idea, what a bogus idea, then a telephone box opened out of nowhere.

'Wicked,' said Ted.

They both saw a man come out of it.

'Hello,' said the man, 'my name is Gash. I came from the box.'

'Where is that?' said Bill

'Just follow me to the box. Don't look, I have typed in a code, 88*46 and here we go,' Gash said.

We were going back in time, but it was still today.

'Where are we?' said Ted.

'We are in the French war.'

'But what about the project for school?'

'Oh yeah, man, we are going to have to get some people for the project.'

They travelled through time and they went and found some people for their project. First they went to get Billy the Kid and Noah and they went to get a Samurai.

Joshua Tyrer-Heath (9)
Stanley Junior School

INTO THE FUTURE

One bright, sunny morning in California, there was a girl called Zoe. She lived with her mum, dad and her big brother Alex. Zoe was 10 and Alex was 12.

Anyway, their mum and dad went out shopping to get some food. Just as their mum and dad had gone, Alex started looking for his Game Boy, which he had left in the cupboard in his bedroom. Just then something fell out from it. It was a little box.
'Come over here,' he shouted.
'Okay,' Zoe shouted back.
They both opened the box and inside was an old clock.
'Wow!' said Alex.
'Big deal,' said Zoe.

Alex carefully lifted the clock out from its box. Then he pushed one of the buttons on the side. Suddenly all they could see were lots and lots of spirals and circles.
'Help!' shouted Zoe.
They felt like they were falling down a very deep, dark hole. But then they stopped falling and landed on the ground with a smack. Alex was the first one to wake up. All around him were big windows and he could see tall, silver buildings outside.
'Zoe,' he said 'wake up.'
'Where are we?' said Zoe sleepily.
'I've got no idea,' said Alex. 'Come on let's get out of this room!'
Instead of a door there was a lift. Zoe pushed a button and a door opened. They stepped inside. Zoe pushed another button. The door shut and the lift went down and down and down and down. Alex and Zoe stepped out of the lift.
'I think we're in the future.' said Zoe, sounding excited.
'Wicked.' said Alex.
They saw lots of people on flying skateboards and in flying cars. Suddenly they saw lots of robots. Alex took the clock out of his pocket. But then he dropped the clock. Before he had time to pick it up a robot got it and put it in his coat pocket.

'Let's follow him.' said Zoe.

They saw the robot put his coat in a spaceship. Zoe and Alex went inside the spaceship and got the clock out of the coat pocket. Suddenly the door shut and they got locked in. They stayed in there for a very long time and as far as I know they're still in there now.

Rebekah O'Connor (9)
Stanley Junior School

THE ALIEN ATTACK

One morning Ben woke up and put his clothes on and ran downstairs. He had some bread rolls with ice cream. Ben jumped on his BMX and went down to the music shop. Ben got a Limp Bizkit song. He put the bag on his arm and went back home.

'Mum, I've got the song!' said Ben.

'OK,' said Mum.

Ben put the music on. The CD was lighting up. Ben was in a spaceship with an alien.

'Help!' said Ben. 'Help! Help! Help! Help! Help! Help! Help *now!'*

'It's OK,' said the little alien. 'My name is Kenny.'

'Where are we?' said Ben.

'In space,' said the little one.

'We can't be in space.'

'Yes we are. I will help you get out of here. But we will go somewhere first, come on!'

'How do you drive this spaceship?'

'Put your cap on!' said the alien.

'OK, off we go!' said Ben. 'Watch out for the rock!'

Bang! We went under the rock that was close.

'We are here, this is my home.'

'Well OK!'

'Hello, my name is Stan.'

'Hello, my name is Catman.'

'Hello, my name is Carl.'

Well I've got an ice cream attack.

'No!' I said. 'Help!'

Stein McGale (9)
Stanley Junior School

178

A Day In The Life Of A Crystal

Hello, my name is Crystal and I'm going to talk about when I was put in a museum. One day I was playing with my friends on the beach. It was very sunny so I was having a great time. Because it was so hot I thought I might go and have a dip in the sea. When I got in there I was cooled off. I got out of the sea and two men were standing there. They picked me up and took me away. I was really scared. They put me in a . . . um, er, Oh I don't know what it's called but they put me in something and drove away. It was very bumpy in the *um* thing. When the men stopped the thing, they took me out and took me to a museum and put me in a cabinet. It was horrible, it was hot and sweaty and the other crystals were really mean and nasty. Lots of people came to the window and stared at all the crystals but not one looked at me. Except for one girl. She looked at me in a very kind way. She said something to me.

She said 'I want to take you back to the beach because I've seen you there.'

I said 'Yes please!' in an excited way.

In the middle of the night I heard something. It was that girl. She took me from the cabinet and took me to her house. The next day she took me to the beach and put me down on the sand.

I said 'Thank you.'

All my friends said 'Where have you been?'

I said 'I will tell you later.'

I hope you enjoyed my story. Goodbye.

Jessie West (9)
Stanley Junior School

A Day In The Life Of A Football

I am a football and I am going to tell you the most miserable day of my life.

I was on the field ready to have a game of football. I heard the whistle and I said to myself 'Oh no!' because I don't like being kicked around. Then I saw David Beckham coming towards me and he took one mighty kick and I went soaring past the net and out of the stadium. I landed with a thud on Connaught Road.

Then someone saw me and came rushing out. She knew who I belonged to, so she went to the police station and said, 'I found this on Connaught Road.'

The police said 'I guess someone kicked it so hard it flew right across to Connaught Road.'

Then the police said that they would return it to them. They returned me to the football club and they said 'Thank you.'

The police said 'We think David Beckham should be in The Guinness Book Of Records.' And so he was. Then they thought that they should put me on display and so they bought a new ball and this is now my new home.

Emily Taylor (9)
Stanley Junior School

A Day In The Life Of My Dog

First, in the morning I wake up and my owners come downstairs. I have my breakfast and a quick walk before my owners go to school (I go with them). When the mum comes back, she takes me to the park. Then we go and pick up the girls. I say hello to them by jumping up at them and then they take me for a walk. Soon after I get back I have a big drink because I get very thirsty after I go for a walk. Then one more of my owners comes back and gives me a walk.

Every time I go for a walk I meet a friend. I have loads of friends. My best friend is a dog called Abbie. I've got more friends, there's Dudley, Honey, Jack and Rolo. Then I go for a walk down the Post Office, go outside, come back in and go to my basket and get to sleep. But when someone is going to bed I say goodnight and I give them a lick.

When Mum and Dad go to bed I go outside and go to the toilet while they block the living room with chairs, shut the door to my dad's computers and put the stair gate up, and then I go to bed.

Alanna Rudd (9)
Stanley Junior School

A Day In The Life Of A Calendar

Hi, my name is Candy Calendar, I am a calendar. My owner is a snotty faced idiot, I positively hate her.

Today is Tuesday and it is 2.30am. My owner is already up, she is writing a love poem to her boyfriend. She is going on a date with him tonight (she wrote that on me). I've seen him before, he came on Sunday. He's just as bad as my owner, he looks like a pig. No, sorry, that was an insult to a pig. He looks worse!

She's coming down now . . . hang on, she wrote something on me. She wrote that she is going on a beauty check-up (ha, ha, ha). Nobody can make her look even the tiniest bit beautiful.

She's writing something else now, it says that she is cancelling her date because she can't get a beauty check-up. Yey!

A few weeks ago the same thing happened. She will be really cross. Anyway, I just love happy endings.

Sarah Perkins (9)
Stanley Junior School

A DAY IN THE LIFE OF A BISCUIT

Hi I'm a tatty old biscuit and I'm going to tell you about the most awful day of my life.

I was lying in my house (a green biscuit tin) and I heard voices saying, 'Come on Liz we're going to the shops, oh grab something to eat will you.'

Just then a big hand came and picked me out of my nice, cosy house. The hand put me in a pocket and when the hand took me out she bit my leg off. Then the hand dropped me on the busy road.

I tried to run off but I was too late. A stream of cars were now rushing past and the big, grey lorry squashed my left arm. A few minutes later, a bright red car knocked me and I rolled, narrowly missing the gutter, onto the pavement and into the nearby park.

On the end of the children's slide was a tramp dressed in checked grey dungarees and a rug around him. He picked me up and was about to eat me when he noticed I had a medium-sized slug on my back which I must have rolled on when I got knocked by that red car. Then the old tramp threw me far away and I landed hard on a very old newspaper, but then I fell into a very hard tin, my new home.

Eva Redman (9)
Stanley Junior School

A Day In The Life Of A Penny

I'm an old penny, been through every till in London. Early on Saturday morning my owner took me out somewhere. My owner took out of his pocket, his cheque book, I was wedged in his cheque book. My owner wrote a cheque for an old man, I slipped out of the cheque book as my owner took it out of his pocket.

I fell into a puddle and sat there for four years, no one noticed me. I got cold and rusty, until a young boy picked me up and popped me into his pocket. That same boy treasured me until he started smoking and had a heart attack. As the boy fell I slipped out of his pocket and crashed on the floor.

One of his caring friends picked me up and took me to his house. The boy plopped me into his money box. I stayed in there for three months until they had a storm with thunder and lightning. It tore the house in half. All of the family got out. The boy took one thing with him, his money box.

He gathered up money for two years and started renting a flat. On they way to his flat one day, the boy hadn't shut his pocket up properly and the money box fell out. The money box smashed. I rolled down the drain, and swam down all the mucky water. When I got to the sewage farm a man was looking through the water for anything good. The man found me and kept me forever. That's how my life went on. I'm old and rusty now.

Ben Hogg (9)
Stanley Junior School

JAMIE'S MAGIC MAYHEM

Whoo-hoo! Jamie danced around the kitchen in total delight, he had just been chosen for the Nathen Talent Contest this evening! Jamie was putting on a magic show. He had practised for weeks and was as excited as ever. He ate his breakfast and went to his room to revise on his work. Jamie was going to use all the advanced pieces of magic to inspire his audience.

It was lunchtime and Jamie was having a short break from his work and checking out his costume that he was going to wear. At last the big night came. He was backstage and as nervous as ever, it was his turn, he got on the stage.

'Ladies and gentlemen, I am here to demonstrate some of the most advanced and cunning acts of magic. Now I need a volunteer from the audience.'
He pointed at a young woman.
'Don't be shy.'
Slowly she stepped onto the stage.
'I will make her into a large box,' he said.
He said 'Shout, 'Nathen Talent Contest'.'
The audience shouted, 'Nathen Talent Contest.'

He opened the door, she was still there, the crowd went quiet. Jamie ran off the stage.

The next morning he woke up with his parents looking at him.
'What happened?' asked Jamie.
'You fainted backstage,' explained his mother.
'It was the shock of everything going wrong. Did I win?'
'No.'
'Oh well, it was worth a try.'

Harry Clayton (9)
Stanley Junior School

AN ALIEN PLAN TO DEFEAT A BULLY

'Squish!' that was the unidentified frying object (in your language it would just be called sausage!)

'Yuck!' that was the cry of dismay that came from poor old Tallis Ceing-Ceang as a helpless little unidentified fry . . . I mean 'sausage', found his grave on Tallis' head!

'Serves you right for tripping up my friend!' That was the voice of a beastly bully named Fuji.
'I've told you a zillion times,' said Tallis, 'it was an accident.'
'Well, it's too late now, I've done it! said Fuji rather quickly.

Tallis started crying. He couldn't believe himself, losing to an alien, twelve inches shorter than he was!

Tallis flew away. He had had enough of this business. Something would have to stop it, but what?

'How can I stop it?' sobbed Tallis to himself. It was then, that he had his great idea . . .

He nervously walked over to Crakker, making sure there was no one about to notice them get together.

Hartley Woolf (9)
Stanley Junior School

GLORY FOR FULHAM

When John Tigerna joined Fulham he changed the team by giving them lots of training. There's only one player who could not stay, it was Kevin Ball. He was a midfielder who played on the left side of the centre. It was Louie Saha who changed the team's fortunes with his amazing goals and skill. Boamorte and Barry Hales are just like Luke Saha but they haven't scored as many goals.

When Tigerna came to Fulham he left the Nationwide Conference to join the Premiership. It was unlucky that Chris Coleman had a car crash just before we played Man United. It was surprising that we had seven players we were meant to have eleven. The score was Man United two, Fulham one. It was a bad day for Fulham supporters although they were looking forward to the day. It was after eighty-five minutes that Manchester United scored and Fulham were out of the finals. They were so unlucky but they still swapped their shirts with United at the end of the game.

Shaun Davis was crying because we were knocked out of the finals. Their home ground is called Craven Cottage. Their kit is black and white. Their away kit is red and white but their new one will be white.

Ben Traverso (9)
Stanley Junior School

ZIGGIZAG AND THE PLANET OF EXPLODING GUNGE MONSTERS

'It is the year 2924,' said the computer in its low metallic voice.
'Yes, I know that but where are we?' said Ziggizag.
'We're at the base you dimwit!' said the computer insultingly.
'Oh yes, I must be losing my memory,' said Ziggizag wearily.

Ziggizag was the captain of Stardust, his spaceship. He worked with his mates Ziggi and Zagga. They had been told to go on a mission to the Planet of Exploding Gunge Monsters!

'How on Stardust are we going to get there?' bellowed Ziggizag.
'Fl . . .fl . . . fly?' stammered Zagga.
'You . . . you . . . nincompoop?' answered Ziggi.
'Yeah, yeah you nincompoop!' muttered Ziggizag.

Suddenly the ground started to rumble.

'Come on you two,' shouted Zagga over the noise of the engine. 'Get on the spaceship.'

So the others hurried on to Stardust and they got started. When they finally reached the planet they were looking for, they stopped and landed Stardust. They were searching an area of the planet when suddenly . . .
'Aaargh!' said something that looked like a green blob.
'Ahem, table manners!' said Ziggi tutting.
'Aaargh!'

The green blob was even angrier and suddenly in a flash attacked Ziggi and also made a strange noise while attacking Ziggi. Suddenly millions and millions of gunge monsters appeared out of the ground.

'Eek, Mummy!' shouted Ziggizag trembling.
'Let's get out of here,' shouted Zagga.

So the three of them raced to Stardust. When they reached the spaceship they got started. Once they were in the middle of their journey something happened.

'Phut, phut, phut, hiss!' the fuel tank had burst but that is another story.

Adam Scott (9)
Stanley Junior School

LUCKY STRIKE

Once there lived a boy with his mother and father in a little town down a valley. The little boy was called David.

David had lots of friends and was very popular! Then one day his mother and father sat around the table and had a little chat with David and said, 'David your father and I want a little talk with you.'
'Why?'
'Because over the past few days your father and I haven't quite got on like we used to.'
'Yes you have. I haven't heard you argue.'
'That's because you're at school all day.'
'So what if you're arguing. What are you going to do about it then?'
'Well your dad and I want a divorce.'
'A divorce! You've got to be kidding. Please Mum, please Dad don't go. Oh no that means only one of you will have me, but which one?'
'That will be me I'm afraid,' David's mum said.

So David went to live with his mum but where did they go? We never knew!

The years passed and we caught up with David and his mum. We asked him if he had any adventures and guess what he said?

'Yes I have and I'll tell you one right now!'

So he did and this is it. When his mother moved from their little town David wandered off and wanted to check out his new environment, he spotted a crocodile and bit him! It wasn't a big adventure but it was one!

Georgina Girling (9)
Stanley Junior School

A DANGEROUS DAY FOR A CHEETAH

It was a normal day. I jumped out of the tree where my last zebra was hidden and started to hunt for my breakfast. When I finally found a herd of zebra, I saw an old male cheetah battling to kill one of them, so I ran over and pounced on the zebra, got hold of its throat and ripped it out.. Then I heard the growl of the old cheetah. I turned round, ripped through the skin, and with half of it, ran off into the tall grass.

When I finally got to a decent tree to hide the zebra in, I climbed it and hid in the very top branches.

Suddenly I heard a yelp and three loud bangs. I looked down and saw two men dragging my sister into a trunk. The anger built up inside me as I saw the truck drive off with my sister. I jumped from the tree and sprinted after the truck, but it was too fast for me to catch up with. Suddenly one of the poachers saw me and used this strange thing that made bangs. Just as a bang noise came from the thing I felt a shooting pain zooming up my leg. I slowed down and saw blood dripping out of my leg. I managed to get away before he did it again. So I ran into the long grass and started to clean my wound.

Daniel Tapson (10)
Stanley Junior School

THE GLAMOROUS LIFE OF GERI HALLIWELL

Tomorrow night from seven till ten o'clock, I've got a massive signing. I arrive in a seven windowed limo. At half-past eight my boyfriend Robbie Williams is coming. I'll be glad to see him.

Recently I've just done 'Raining Men' for the 'Bridget Jones's Diary' sound track and Robbie's done a song as well.

I was in competition with Emma Bunton when she did 'What I Am Is, What I Am' and I did 'Lift Me Up' and I made number one and she made number two in the hit parade.

Since I left the Spice Girls I've had a new look. I've lost weight and I've got blonder hair. I feel much better about myself as well.

Some days are better than others as sometimes fans come screaming up to me. I mean it's wonderful to see them but sometimes it gets quite annoying. But some fans are very polite and just come up to me and shake my hand.

Tomorrow night when I get back from the signing all I will want to do is go to bed and eat Ben and Jerry ice cream, it's my favourite ice cream in the whole wide world. Well I'd better be getting my beauty sleep.

Bethany Shannahan (9)
Stanley Junior School

A Day In The Life Of A Frog

I was preparing to hatch out of the spawn. I was getting ready for what was going to happen next. Then I popped out of the spawn, it wasn't at all what I thought it would be. It was all cold, wet and scary. I then started moving my tail and I moved it so much I was off in no time. I started to swim around. I found lots of other tadpoles that looked like me, so I tried to go over but they just swam away. I went to the other side of the big pond where I smelt fear. Suddenly I saw a big eel swimming towards me.

'Swim,' I said. 'Swim.'

I swam as fast as I could. I hid in a small crack in a big rock. The eel bashed his head very badly on the rock, so he swam away. I sneaked out of the rock and looked for a safer place to hide. I found myself back at the same place. I looked back and saw two little legs pop out of my tail. Oh no, what was happening? Suddenly another tadpole came out of the dark and the same thing had happened to him. He told me to relax and that it was meant to happen. He told me that soon I would get some arms too and also change to green. Then I would be called a frog.

Kareem Al Abd (10)
Stanley Junior School

A DAY IN THE LIFE OF RONAN KEATING

I woke up this morning feeling nervous about tonight. I think I'm number one for the 10th week, so I will be singing on 'Top of the Pops' again this Saturday. I've got a problem though, I don't know what to wear. I might wear the clothes I normally wear, that is my jeans jacket, leather trousers and my white shirt.

The show starts at 6.00pm and I will catch my private jet at 5.00pm from Dublin. When I get to London Richard Blackwood will pick me up from the airport so he can take me to the 'Top of the Pops' studio. I rehearse my song and have my favourite background all perfect. I am going to be the last one to sing because I am number one.

I am very nervous, it is nearly my turn to go on stage to perform my number one song. I am going on stage now to sing 'Lovin' Each Day'. Finally I have finished my song. I am very happy because I can now give some more money to charities in Southern Ireland. So goodnight everybody in Ireland and England. I might see you on 'Top of the Pops' next week.

Paul Hennessy (10)
Stanley Junior School

Middy's Day Out

I woke up early feeling jumpy and excited. I put on my ragged, pink dress as I was going down the rabbit hole I spotted yesterday.

I quickly ran over the mole hills, then I quickly jumped down the rabbit hole.

I squeezed down the hole, it was dark and creepy and looked like it had been untouched for weeks. The hole kept going and going but eventually I saw a circle of light above me. At the time I was exhausted but I kept going. Finally I reached the top.

Outside I hastily ran into a berry bush trying not to get pricked. I sat there hesitantly when suddenly I heard a voice shout, 'Hey, there's something in the bushes over there, quick grab a net.'
'Aargh,' I squealed but it was too late. The poachers had caught me.

A filthy, vicious poacher roughly put me into a net and then he put me in a dark, crammed cardboard box. I closed my eyes and I hoped it was a dream, then I fell asleep.

I woke up with a fright as I had had a horrible dream. It was about me being in a really big maze and I couldn't escape from these tigers chasing me. Suddenly a hand opened the box and picked me up by the scruff of the neck. The poacher put me on a splintery table. He poked me with a sharp stick. I started to bleed.

'Ah this badger is no good,' said the poacher.

He put me in the box again and set me free outside. I quickly ran down the hole but I was still bleeding in pain.

I finally arrived at my little house and as I was so exhausted I quickly fell asleep in my old armchair peacefully and quietly.

Emma Formstone (10)
Stanley Junior School

A DAY IN THE LIFE OF OMY THE OTTER

I saw the sun glint off those huge scales. The slimy body of this creature appeared here and there in my beloved river, with hardly a ripple or a splash, it just seemed to slide towards me. Closer, closer . . . those terrifying eyes, glowing yellow.

'No! Please! Noooo!'

Bump!

Ouch! I saw stars for a moment, and then I realised where I was. My slim figure was sprawled on the floor next to my bed. I was having nightmares again! Still sweating with fear, I got up and waddled out for a wash.

I was still trying to figure out the meaning of my dream when I was on my daily wander for berries and nuts when I saw it. Up on a small hill, I could quite clearly see some humans in a contraption that they call a boat, on my river!

I decided to get as much information as I could, which would mean having to get a closer look.

On my way, I noticed that some snare traps had been set, humans!

I jumped in the river and swam home unaware of the new positions of the humans and their nets!

Something caught my tail and pulled me up! The next thing I knew I was hanging upside down by a hook, fear overcame me and I just blacked out.

They must have put me back in the water because when I awoke, I was on a completely different bank!

That place we made our home and lived there away from trouble, but what we didn't notice was the yellow bulldozer on the horizon . . .

Andrew Wilson (10)
Stanley Junior School

A Day In The Life Of A Panda

I was in a bamboo forest. I am a panda. My babies are two weeks old. I am struggling to survive. I could hear footsteps coming closer and closer. I was crunching on bamboo when I heard the deafening sound of bamboo being sawn down.

Afterwards I realised they were here to cut down the whole bamboo wood! This is why there are very few of us pandas. They keep cutting down all our bamboo!

I crept out of the bamboo woods to get away from the humans. When I came back all that was left were tiny stumps of bamboo. Not enough to live on. My heart sank.

What was I going to do? How was I going to stay alive? I had no food, I had nothing. I just sat there waiting and waiting. It had been five days. I was very weak from starvation. As the days pass I got weaker and weaker. Finally I could take no more and I died.

The sound of the saw is still a piercing reminder of the day they cut the bamboo forest down - I never knew what happened to my babies and I never will.

Laura Spencer (10)
Stanley Junior School

A DAY IN THE LIFE OF TONY BLAIR

I woke up, it was the day before the election. It felt like half my body was excited, and the other half was nervous. I got dressed in my smart suit, and went downstairs. I made my way to the Houses of Parliament. It was really nerve-racking as we had to practise our speeches. As the day passed on I went back to 10 Downing Street in my posh car. I felt so tired I went upstairs to bed, but it was very difficult to sleep because I was really excited.

The next morning I jumped out of bed, today was the day of the election. My tummy felt like it had butterflies in it. It was a very funny feeling. I went downstairs and switched on the telly. I saw all the votes flooding in, it was really tense. Suddenly the votes stopped. I looked at the scores, Charles Kennedy had 1599 votes, I had 1598, I was two away from winning the election. Just then, two more votes came in for me, I had won the election! I felt so relieved I was going to be Prime Minister for another year. It was a really good feeling. I rushed into the kitchen, hugged and kissed my wife. From that day forward I will always remember the day of the election in 2001.

Alexander Hankey (10)
Stanley Junior School

A Day In The Life Of A Tiger

Hi, I'm Tiny the Tiger. You're probably thinking I'm tiny because of my name, well you're right. I'm a baby tiger and I've only just learnt how to catch my dinner. It was a bit complicated the way my mum was telling me.

She kept on saying, 'Oh you're crouched down too much,' or 'don't worry you'll get it some day.' Sometimes when she keeps on blabbering away I forget what the most important part is.

One day I finally caught a deer. It was very nice but it was a hot day, so I relaxed and didn't eat much. My mum helped me kill it but I was the one who grabbed it.

She's yapping away at the deer right now. I think catching my prey isn't easy when you've got your mum telling you what to do all the time. Anyway, I'm going to practice some more tomorrow.

Mum's catching our midnight snack tonight - even though she always does. I'm going to sleep after my snack - I hope it's a smaller deer because the deer I caught was a little too big.

Umm, this deer is tasty, I'll just have another bite. Crunch! Whoops! Maybe I crunched that a bit too much. Well, I'm really sleepy, tired and weary. Goodnight everyone. Have some happy and exciting dreams.

Lucy Tyrell (10)
Stanley Junior School

A Day In The Life Of Robbie Williams

I woke up thinking about my performance. I sat down thinking about the order of my songs. As I was doing that I was getting quite nervous just like Neil Armstrong landing on the moon for the first time. I was excited as well. I kept thinking, only one more sleep until I perform. I am going to perform my new song, 'Supreme'. I was hoping they would like it. I had to ring my organiser to check everything was going to plan and my director. I had to go to the stage arena to help with the set up. The stage was a bit boring. I wanted lights, bright lights. When we had finished it looked brilliant. Then I had a full rehearsal. When I got back to my hotel I was all set and ready to go.

Today is the day, the day of my performance. When I'd got all my clothes together I waited for my limo to take me to the stage. I had all my make-up and changed into baggy jeans and a T-shirt. I could hear the crowd converging like a herd of elephants.

'This is the moment you have been waiting for, the one, the only, Robbie Williams!'

Caine Marshall (10)
Stanley Junior School

A Day In The Life Of A Squirrel

Five days ago I was searching for food when I heard a noise, a loud noise. The tree I was next to seemed to be coming closer. I suddenly realised it was falling. I nipped away as quickly as I could but the end of my tail was torn.

As my tail was torn I couldn't balance as well, so it was hard to walk. As I looked up, I could see three giant humans. One had a chainsaw and the other two had axes.

'Oh no,' I thought, 'they're going to kill me!'

Luckily they were starting on the tree behind me, but what I didn't know was that the tree behind me was my home. So I just ran away to the playhouse tree.

I stopped on the way wondering if my wife was alright on her own (but of course she was killed by the chainsaw). As I arrived I was disgusted. The playhouse tree had been cut down too.

'Why, though? Why?' I said. 'I'd better go to Badger.'

Badger was my wisest friend. As I made my way on through the forest, I got caught in a tin can. I was stuck for a good few hours, but then it was just too much for me. The top of the can was sharp so I had deep cuts and I was starving.

So in the end all was still, I was still, I was dead.

Oliver Baum (10)
Stanley Junior School

A Day In The Life Of Bertie The Horse

Morning

Today I woke up later than usual, but I didn't mind, that meant I already had my oats waiting for me. I gobbled them down and waited for Clair to notice I was awake. I was happy, after all today is my last day of labour for three months! Clair led me out of my stable with a leading rein and tied it to the gate near Ebony. Then she started mucking out my stable, when she was finished she got out what I call 'the painful process', the clippers!

No way was she coming near me with those vicious instruments! She came towards me and started to clip me. I bucked! Crash! I had knocked down the stone wall! Luckily cloudy wasn't in his stable, but I still got the blame!

Afternoon

I went to Bushy Park. Emma rode me and we went through the river! It's fun at the time but the hair on my hooves gets all matted.

Evening

Clair tried to brush me. I tossed about but she got me, and it wasn't too bad. Well, not as bad as you-know-what! She brushed my hair down, and now I have a big tuft of hair on my belly!

Night

Today was a busy one. Tomorrow I'll go into the field! I can't wait! I'm as excited as a child on a fast ride, but as Emma says, still as hairy as Bertie! You know, I may have been chased by the clippers, and get my hair matted so that it had to be brushed! But at the end of the day everybody can find something to put a smile on their face.

Rebecca Shaw
Stanley Junior School

A Day In The Life Of Britney Spears

Beep, beep, beep, beep went my alarm clock this morning. As I reached over to turn it off I remembered that I had to finish off my song.

I got out of bed and got changed into my clothes. After breakfast I walked down to the recording studios to finish my new song, 'Stronger'.

It was still only seven o'clock when I finished my song. Now to record it, I thought to myself.

I felt really proud and a little nervous when the record company said my song was brilliant. It made me more confident for when I sang my song in front of the producer.

When I had sung to him, and had recorded my song, I got into my limousine and went home.

When I got back to my house there was a message on the answerphone. It was a radio station ringing up to see if I could appear on their show. I felt very anxious as I phoned them up and said I could.

I felt as empty as a car with no petrol, so I just crashed out on the sofa.

It was the end of another long, hard day. I was dreaming about playing at my concert in Paris in a few weeks time.

Louise Peppis-Whalley (9)
Stanley Junior School

A Day In The Life Of Nelson Mandela

I woke up, it was dawn. I thanked the house owner and slipped silently into the oncoming light. I ran quietly through the streets, my heart pounding like a big bass drum gone out of control.

Should I carry on with my protest? I already had the authorities after me!

No, I would carry on! I turned a corner and knocked on a door. It creaked open and an old lady appeared in the doorway dressed in a shawl, thin jumper and an odd pair of socks. She gave me a strange look, then beckoned and I followed her inside. She closed the door quietly behind her.

'You want hiding?' she said in a croaky voice.
'If you can,' I said a touch sheepishly.
'Follow me,' and she led me into a second room.

In there, there was only a dusty rug. She dragged it away to reveal a trapdoor, she lifted it and I walked down the stairs. I listened to her put the door back and replace the rug, and I was plunged into darkness. I dropped against the hard stone wall and fell asleep.

I was woken some hours later by loud hammering on the door. I heard it creak open.

Police!

Sean Julliard (9)
Stanley Junior School

A Day In The Life Of A White Tiger

I'm a seven year old white tiger called Told. I've just woken up and I'm shattered because I had a very exciting day yesterday. My mum's gone out somewhere, and that leaves me to hunt for food for myself. I'm just going to hunt a zebra, but I have to be extremely quiet.

There they are near the bushes. I'm going to run after three. One . . . two . . . three. There I've got one. No! The pack are coming. I'm really nervous because they told me that if I caught a zebra, or any other creature and didn't tell them about it, they would take all my food away and eat it. They're coming closer and closer and they've just missed. Phew!

Do you want to know how I'm feeling? Well relieved, because the pack missed me and happy because I met up with Gode, my best friend.

'Look out!' he screamed.

Two hunters were after us and Gode has been shot by a gun, and they're now after me. I've lost them. I'm panting as quickly as a dog.

It's now night-time and my mum's got home and I've told her about my day. She was sad that Gode is probably dead and happy that the pack didn't catch me. My mum's got a cut from glass left by thoughtless tourists and I'm happy that she's come home. Goodnight.

Tristan Loffler (10)
Stanley Junior School

A Day In The Life Of Sara The Hamster

Hi, I'm Sara. Can I tell you how I got to this place? I will start here.

One day a girl and three other people walked into my home, at least I thought it was. Anyway, the girl pointed at my brother, but she didn't want him. After the man put my brother back, she pointed at me. The man picked me up and put me in a box. Suddenly something started moving. About twenty minutes later we stopped. The girl took me out of the box and put me in a cage. It was horrible. I was so scared.

After a while, the girl picked me up and hugged me. She even gave me a name, Sara.

One year later I bit the girl twice. I thought she was food. It looked like food, but it didn't taste like food. I don't know why I did it. The girl didn't hold me again. I thought she was frightened of me.

After two years, something strange happened to me. I was just lying there. A woman put on a pair of gloves and picked me up. She put me in a plastic bag and threw it away.

I don't know why I've got a white dress on and a circle over my head. I just want to be with the girl again.

Carly Clarke (10)
Stanley Junior School

A Day In The Life Of My Hamster, Cookie

It is Wednesday 9th May. I am going home from the vets. Ahh someone's coming over to get one of us. Oh, she's picking me up, I think this means I am going home. Yes there's my dad (Chris). The first things he says are, 'Hello Cookie are you alright now?'

I wished I could say I'm say but I can't speak. It was quite a long and bumpy journey home but we made it. Dad tried to put me straight in to the living room of my house but I stupidly jumped out of his hand and off the drawers where my home was. He then thought it would be safer on the floor, so my house is there now.

I just had a normal day after that until my dad wanted to hold me. It took him quite a long time to get me out, then he held me and put me in my ball. After he put me back in my house but he didn't realise he had left the sleeping compartments lid lose. I decided to wait until he was asleep, since it was 9.45pm, then I pushed off the lid and got out. I didn't realise that once I had got out someone else would have to put me back in my house. Anyway when Dad woke up the lid was off so he started looking around. Then I saw him looking at me, they put some treats in my ball and I couldn't resist it.

Christopher McLaughlin (10)
Stanley Junior School

A DAY IN THE LIFE OF GRAHAM THORPE

I have chosen Graham Thorpe, a very good cricket player. I have chosen the day when England played Pakistan because he played brilliantly.

England lost the toss and Pakistan wanted to bowl. After England had lost three wickets it was Graham Thorpe's turn to bat and the other batsman was Nasser Hussain. Both Graham Thorpe and Nasser Hussain batted very well, they kept on getting fours and twos. Then Graham Thorpe got his fifty. It was hard work but eventually he got his eighty but unfortunately three overs later he was bowled out. As he walked back to the balcony the crowd gave him a huge round of applause. After England were bowled out it was Pakistan's turn to bat.

Pakistan were four wickets down when Graham Thorpe made his first of four spectacular catches. It was a low diving catch but he managed to catch it. About forty-five minutes later when England really needed a wicket they got one more from another wonderful diving catch from Graham Thorpe. England had not taken a wicket for a long time until Graham Thorpe took a superb catch in the last half an hour. Finally in the last ten minutes Graham Thorpe caught his fourth catch and that was the match winner. So England had won the first test match against Pakistan. After the match Graham Thorpe was awarded the 'Man of the Match'. England won the game by a day's innings and nine runs. Another great day for a great cricketer.

Pablo Shah (9)
Stanley Junior School

MY DOG EDDY

I chose my dog Eddy because I always, always play with him and he is special.

I think he is very, very much fun to play with. He likes playing with a ball. He makes me laugh. He is only four years old. Loads and loads of people like him because he is popular. Everyone calls him Edd because that is his short name but I call him Eddy.

I don't see him every day. I see him like every year. This year I think I will see him. He lives in Bosnia with my auntie. I could take him with me to England but I can't, it's a real shame, isn't it? He is a male. I am going to train him all sorts of stuff like rolling over. I also bought him a ball to chase as a present.

Anel Kahrimanovic (10)
Stanley Junior School

A DAY IN THE LIFE OF DANNY FROM HEAR'SAY

This morning my alarm went off at 6.30. I had a lot of rehearsing to do. I had a big day ahead of me at the Brits. I dashed downstairs and gulped down breakfast. I met Noel, Kym, Myleene and Suzanne who already practising dance moves in the studio. The crew were practising different camera angles and shots for the TV programme Popstars. After a vigorous half hour of energetic dance moves we got a five minute break to discuss any new dance moves.

I rang up my mum and told her to watch the Brits and tell her I was practising hard. At 12.30 we rang up and got a takeaway pizza before starting to practise again. It was 3.30pm and we went to meet up with Nicki Chapman, Paul Adams and Nigel Lythgoe. We performed our No 1 hit single 'Pure And Simple' with all the new added dance moves to them. After three and a half hours of rehearsing, only stopping for supper, we travelled to the Brits, arriving at 7.20pm. We immediately went to makeup and then went to the costume room. At 7.45pm we were ready to go! What a day!

Jonathan Littledale (10)
Stanley Junior School

THE DAY IN THE LIFE OF A T-REX

The huge body of the T-rex bent over to drink the cool clean water of the lagoon. His body was towering over the small procomsognathus triassicus. It was probably going to be the last drink he would take before he reached the mating ground. At best it would take him the rest of the day to get there. He started prodding in his awkward way. Soon he came to the top of a cliff. From there he could see the mating ground, a good fifteen miles off. He thought it would not take him long to get there. But how wrong he was .He then heard a sound that made him shudder. It was the sound of a rival male. The rival rex rammed against him nearly knocking him off the cliff. Our rex started running as hard as he could. When he looked behind, he saw that the rival had taken a different route. Soon he saw the mating ground about two hours off. What is that, is it a water hole? he thought. It was. He drunk the cool refreshing water. Then he saw fire, heard a bang, then blackness.

Louis Archer (9)
Stanley Junior School

A Day In The Life Of A White Siberian Tiger

I had been taking a mid-morning nap, in the cool shade of the Mandlebrack tree, when a blood-curdling gun shot woke me up. In my curiosity, I carefully padded along to the clearing of the forest.

Poachers! The poachers were both large, bulky men with thick, black eyebrows and greasy moustaches. I hid my snowy face amongst the grass, hoping to be missed. Indian poachers were rare in Siberia, but they were also the worst. They shot tigers like me, and skinned them for their fur.

I was about to creep away into the depths of the forest, when one of the poachers turned his head and saw me! I ran, panic-stricken and my mind racing, as the poachers aimed their fire at me. They got me once, on the paw, but I carried on, my wound throbbing.

I had finally reached my home, a grey cave covered in snow and the entrance hidden by a gigantic snow-drift. I dived in, and the leaves shook, blowing a chilly breeze across my face. I stood perfectly still, as the poachers trudged past my hiding place, cursing because they had lost me.

Once I was sure that the poachers had gone, I gently licked my injured paw. It stung, and as I winced, I noticed for the first time in a long while, that I was hungry, so I began a weary hunt for food.

After devouring a hairy, but juicy monkey, I was feeling remarkably tired, so I lay down, my eyes dropping, and I fell into a deep sleep.

Kaori Takenaka (10)
Stanley Junior School

A Day In The Life Of A Two Pound Coin

I started off in a big, big bag. I got dumped in a truck with a lot of other coins.

'Argh!' I cried, but no one heard me as my muffled voice disappeared.

I found myself in a large counter with a cheerful crowd of two pound coins. A huge hand came down and picked me up. I was handed over to a fat lady's hand and put in a sleek tiger skin purse, with a richly decorated clasp.

My new owner was walking down the street when she stopped at a phone box, got out her purse and put some money in. A small child picked me up and put me in his pocket and quietly ran away.

I was in this boy's piggy bank when I heard some weird, but loud noises. There was a huge crash and a smashing of glass. A burglar! I was grabbed with a large group of other things and shaken about.

'Yuck!' I shouted.

The burglar had given me to his baby son and he had put me in his mouth!

I heard some strange sound as the baby was rushed to hospital. I was stuck!

I was prodded with tools until I arrived out. The surgeon washed me in disinfectant and put me in his pocket.

Later on I was spent and landed in the same counter I had been in that morning! Isn't life strange!

What an exhausting day!

Alex Dehnel (10)
Stanley Junior School

A DAY IN THE LIFE OF QUEEN ELIZABETH (COMING INTO REIGN)

I have chosen Queen Elizabeth (coming into reign) because I know a lot about her and we have been studying her in class. I have chosen her because I wanted to write a detailed piece of writing.

It was the year 1558 and I, Elizabeth had just got up, I dressed whilst I thought what lay ahead in the day. I went downstairs and saw breakfast on the table. I sat down on a chair and ate very slowly, I could feel something wonderful was going to happen. After I was finished I went out into the gardens, it was a beautiful day and the sun was shining brightly. I went back in to get a book then I went and sat under a tree. I started to read, five minutes later I heard the sound of hooves, I looked up, I saw three men on horseback. The middle one was holding the crown. I knew what was going to happen, they all knelt in front of me and proclaimed me Queen of all England, I wanted to cry but did not. I said this in Latin, 'God has brought this upon me. I shall wear the crown with honour.'

Then a horse was fetched for me from the stable, and I rode with them to the palace of Westminster. By the time we got there it was dark, and I went to bed feeling very content that I had the chance to rule at last.

David Fairbairn (10)
Stanley Junior School

THE DAY IN MY LIFE WHICH WAS THE WORST EVER

Dear Diary, I live in an old broken down house in the countryside with Ben the child and Sarah the mother. It is a cold day here in Liverpool and everyone is feeling miserable. Today was a terrible day for me, Michael the mouse.

At the start of the day I was woken up by Ben's alarm clock falling on the floorboard where I live. It was horrible, the end of the floorboard came springing up, and my bed which is placed on it went flying up into the air.

For breakfast I had four cherry stones (my favourite), a core of an apple and a fish bone, (nothing wasted!) After breakfast there was another mishap, the cleaner. I had just finished breakfast in a happy mood, when out came the floor polishing bottle and a scrubbing brush. Help. I was almost drowned with soap bubbles. It wasn't over yet. I remembered that it was a Tuesday and the cleaner stayed for a whole three hours. I went through it all. Rubbish collecting (all my food gone). The Hoover messing up my whole home and making it stick to the ceiling! When I thought it was all over and I had had enough, I decided to have a nap in one of the duvets. It was very crowded in the duvet, I found two wood lice, a spider and my worst enemy Rachel rat! Just as I thought things couldn't get worse the duvet started shaking from side to side, up and down. The cleaner was making the beds!

In the evening I went to Scotland staircase shoe shop to buy some new shoes when I head Sarah saying to Ben
'Are you ready for moving out, Ben? DJ's already here!'
I was dumbstruck, a man in his thirties came walking in, there was a deafening sound coming out of the box he was holding. *Oh help,* I thought.

Hayley Gardiner (9)
Stanley Junior School

A Day In The Life Of Graham Thorpe

I have chosen Graham Thorpe because he is a brilliant cricket player; he scored eighty runs against Pakistan.

I woke up. Today was the big day. England were playing Pakistan in cricket; I was playing for England. I quickly got changed and ran to catch the cricket team bus. I caught it just in time, for the rest of my team wwas already there. It was a long, bumpy journey to the cricket stadium. I was so nervous I was shaking. The crowd roared as loud as a thousand canon balls shooting off at the same time!

The Pakistan team were coming out from the other end of the cricket stadium. England were batting first, and I was batting second. The first batsman only scored ten runs. I was next; fear was taking me over. The bowler looked at me and smiled. He bowled the ball as hard as he could. I almost missed it but I just hit the ball with the edge of my bat. The ball went soaring over the stadium and landed fifty feet away from me. I ran thirty times without stopping. The next bowl was a bit lighter and I whacked the ball as hard as I could. The ball almost got stuck in the top of the stadium. This time I ran fifty times. I batted again but this time I was caught out. We finally won ninety runs to fifty runs. When I got back on the bus, my team cheered me as loudly as I could imagine. I was as pleased as I had ever been in my life.

Max Effendowicz (9)
Stanley Junior School

A Day In The Life Of Dennis The Hamster

Dennis the hamster was sleeping soundly when he was jerked awake by a loud rumble. It seemed to be getting nearer until it stopped, Suddenly there was a crunch coming from above. He poked his nose out of his sawdust bed and clambered out then out, out of nowhere a huge hand grabbed him. Dennis frantically wriggled about but the hand was too strong. He gave a squeak as he was thrust into a cardboard tube, Dennis was in total darkness until at last he came out of the other end.

He heard voices in a very strange language
'Tea's ready!'
'OK, I'm coming.'
He was put back in his cage, when the footsteps died away he looked up and saw that the cage lid wasn't on properly. He began to jump up at it. After a while he managed to grab hold of the rim of the cage and scrambled out onto the floor. When he looked up he saw the most feared creature by hamsters, a cat! It picked him up in its great jaw. Then he heard the thunderous footsteps again. Suddenly the cat dropped him. Once again the huge hand grasped him and shoved him back in his cage. He looked at the cat and stuck his tongue out at it and went back to sleep.

Jack Schofield (10)
Stanley Junior School

A DAY IN THE LIFE OF IAN THORPE

'Bring, bring'! The alarm sounded at 5am. 'Oh no, not another gruelling day of swimming training,' I thought to myself, but suddenly I remembered it was the Sydney Olympics 2000!

'Ian,' shouted Mum, 'come downstairs, it's time to get on the plane.'

I rushed downstairs and got into the coach which drove me to the airport where I met up with the rest of the team. I got onto the plane and soon we were soaring up into the sky. In the plane my thoughts were all about the gun, and off I would go, but that was still to come in real life. We eventually landed at Sydney airport after a long flight from Canberra.

The time came; we marched into a magnificent and huge stadium. Everyone was cheering us in, we were the home country. Cathy Freeman went up and lit the torch. After a good rest I was ready for anything coming - other swimmers and a cold pool!. Luckily the pool was warm and I was fine. First came the relay and we won that and also broke a new record. Second came the one hundred metres freestyle. I won that, then the two hundred freestyle and finally the one hundred and fifty freestyle. I just won that ahead of Edwin Vandonal.

My mum used to say I had such big feet that shoes could never fit me, but she can't laugh about my size 17 feet now can she?

Scott Jermy (10)
Stanley Junior School

ROCK STAR INVASION

One sunny, summer's morning, Frank woke up with his alarm clock beeping loudly across the table. Slowly he got up and crawled over to the TV and turned it on and crept back to his bed. He started flicking through the channels until he suddenly stopped at an interview on Craig David. He'd forgot that it was Saturday so he put his school uniform on, but then he saw the date on the TV and changed into his casual clothes. Just then his mum called him.

'Frank, come down here, your father wants you.' He started to trudge downstairs and said, 'What?'

'Son, there's a package for you here.'

'What?'

'Look it's here.'

'Wow!'

'Open it Frank.'

He opened it and there were two tickets to see an Eminem concert on 19.7.01.

'This is amazing, I'm going to see Eminem today.'

'Wait Frank there's more, there's also a slip for you to go to a rock star teacher.'

'Let me see that, wow!'

He ran upstairs singing, 'I'm going to be a rock star.' About an hour later he was watching Eminem and came back home. Then he went to that rock star place and had a nice teacher called Blateman. He never knew this, but he was good at it.

Blateman let him enter a small competition for mini rock stars. When he got there he was nervous because he was against him. When it was his turn, he was playing a tune called 'Aliens Have Come'. He was about half-way through when a spaceship smashed through the roof and a voice said, 'We're going to take over your planet.'

'Oh no!'

Edward Allinson (9)
Stanley Junior School

THE GHOST AND THE GORGON

One night my little sister went to bed. She doesn't like going to bed. Her name is Anabelle.

That night, when everybody was in bed, she heard a big noise, like a bomb, but it wasn't. She saw a big white sheet like a ghost. She got a fork and threw it at the ghost. The ghost flew out the window. Anabelle didn't get to sleep. She shut the window fast.

The next night arrived. Anabelle slept with her mum. Luckily the ghost didn't come that night for it was dead, but you don't know the other thing they had in store . . . a gorgon, a blue and green monster, a yellow monster, a red monster, a grey monster and so on and another ghost to scare her more.

The night after, she slept in her own bed. She was really scared. The grey monster came to scare her, he was the second most powerful monster. She had to kill him and the gorgon.

Six nights of killing monsters. There was only one left. The gorgon came but this was a bit different, *she had more heads.* Six or seven heads she had, but luck came, she killed it.

Alice Wilson (9)
Stanley Junior School

GOING BACK TO GREECE

Hi I am Edmund Croall, well I am writing about a very strange thing that happened to me.

It all started when I was six and a half. I was staying in an old castle with my grandma. I was exploring when I saw a passageway or to be precise, a secret passageway. I walked down the secret passageway and I saw a door. There was a sign on the door which said *LAB* in big bold letters. I opened the door and there was a laboratory! In the laboratory there was a curtain. On the curtain there was a little stitching which said to me *machine*. I opened the curtain and there was a little room. The little room had a screen and a few buttons. I saw a button that said *Hercules* and another button that said *Ancient Greece*. I pressed both buttons then suddenly, I was whizzing around.

Two minutes later I found myself against a rock. I saw a lion. I thought to myself, I must be Hercules and this is ancient Greece and I had better *run!* I ran as fast as I could but the lion chased me. I plucked up some courage and I made a swipe at the lion and managed to cut its head off but another two heads appeared so I had to cut them off but then another two heads came back. So I cut off the four heads with my sword and then hit them with my club. I had killed the lion.

Suddenly, I was whizzing back to the modern world. *Bump!* I was back at the castle and back in my room.

Edmund Croall (9)
Stanley Junior School

A DAY IN THE LIFE OF NEIL HODGSON

'Go!' the flag was up. All I could hear under the helmet was revving as everyone got ready for the big race. We were coming to the first corner on the second lap. I concentrated hard because corners were the most difficult part of the race.

Suddenly I skidded on the third corner. *Crash, bang, wallop!* All the agony shot through my body. I had slid on a bit of gravel and I had spun off the track. I chucked my bike on the grass and I walked back to the pits. I was so angry because I had not seen the gravel. It should not have been there.

I went to find out who was responsible, I spoke to the car racers who had been racing before us, they did not know anything about the gravel. So I went to see the man who changed the rubber on the tracks and he said he had not see the bit of gravel.

I knew I could have won the race if there had not been any gravel. I would make sure there would be no gravel in the next race and I would get my place back.

Tom Ashby (10)
Stapleford Primary School

A DAY IN THE LIFE OF A GUINEA PIG

'This is the life!' I sighed, 'what are we doing today?' I strolled out of my pen with Rowdy (my pal) behind me. We were only out in the cool, morning garden for two minutes when suddenly a huge crow invited himself into our garden. Rowdy and I ran as fast as our little legs could carry us. It was no good - our lovely, sunny Sunday afternoon turned into a disaster. 'Eeeaak!' Rowdy and I squealed as loudly as our voice boxes could vibrate. We had been injured.

Our owner came to our rescue with a look of horror on his face. The next thing we knew, we were in a cardboard box being rushed to the vets. We squealed and screeched to be let out. We both hated the vet. She pulls your fur and sticks pointy things into your skin.

It was so embarrassing, both of us had to have a stupid cone around our necks to stop us licking the wounds, I mean how pathetic is that.

It was in the afternoon that the most extraordinary thing happened. The same huge, black as ink crow visited us again. This time the story was different. Instead of the crow scaring us we scared him by frightening him off with our cones. We held our large tummies and chuckled with joy. I was sure that I would remember this tragic day for many years to come.

Samantha Harris (11)
Town Farm Primary School

A Day In The Life Of Santa

'I wish I was Santa Claus,' shouted Douglas, 'he doesn't have to do any work!' but as he said that, the room began to shake. He twirled to the North Pole, (it was only two days before Christmas). He looked around and saw two little elves and they asked, 'Hello Santa, got the toys ready yet?' Douglas was bewildered. Was he really Santa?

Later that morning the toy machine broke down. Douglas was frozen solid and the bright light hurt his eyes. 'Oh no!' he screeched, 'It's broken!' Yes, now he wasn't so sure he wanted to be Santa. The toy machine was the only way of making toys, so without it he was desperate. No more toys could be made, but with a little help from the elves (and a sledgehammer), the machine was soon fixed which made Douglas feel much better. Time flew by once the machine was fixed and Douglas wasn't so stressed.

'I like being Santa, but I want to go home now,' Douglas thought to himself. He was very pleased for coping so well as being Santa. The next morning Douglas woke up and found a note by his bed saying, 'Sorry about the broken toys, Love Santa.' Douglas was thrilled with himself and chuffed that Santa had done a lot for him. Douglas had also learnt to not judge a book by its cover because no matter how simple the job may seem there is always a downside.

Catherine Lesley (10)
Town Farm Primary School

A Day In The Life Of Santa

'I knew I shouldn't have eaten that extra mince pie,' moaned Santa as he struggled to climb out of the sleigh, 'haven't we been to this house yet?' He staggered over to the chimney. The roof was slippery and the night sky was as black as ink. It was freezing cold, 'Well I better get on with my job,' cried Santa, as he walked over to the chimney, where he noticed that it hadn't been cleaned.

He attempted to climb down it but got stuck. 'Oh no! What if I am stuck here forever?' Santa began to think, 'I know, I'll call the EEL (Emergency Elf Line)!' He grabbed his mobile phone and rang them. They suddenly arrived in no time. The two elves were on a mission to save Santa.

They grabbed his hands and struggled to pull him out. Eventually he popped out. They helped him finish his job and made sure he ate no more mince pies. Santa realised that every cloud has a silver lining and was grateful of the EEL and will never eat too many mince pies and maybe go on a diet. 'What a Christmas Eve,' Santa said with a sigh of relief.

Douglas Clayton (10)
Town Farm Primary School

A DAY IN THE LIFE OF A SNOWMAN

'Mu, Mum, wake up!'

'Why?'

'It's been snowing.' Ben put all of his warmest clothes on and shot out of the house like a bullet. A few hours later he came in and had built the most wonderful snowman. It was now suppertime and his snowman still looked as good as when Ben had first made it. It was now bedtime and Ben didn't want to see his snowman melt, so in the middle of the night he got up, looked out of his window and gazed at the snowman.

Then all of a sudden a light shone down on the snowman and he started to move. Ben rushed downstairs and thought that it was the best moment of his entire life. The snowman said to the boy, 'We can go wherever you want as long as it's somewhere cold.' So off they went to find the coldest places all over the world (Iceland and Switzerland).

They finally arrived home and the sun started to rise and the snowman said, 'Well it's time for me to go.' And with that the snowman gradually started to melt. The boy felt sad, but he knew that whenever he saw snow he would remember the amazing snowman and their fantastic adventures around the world.

Samuel Chesterman (10)
Town Farm Primary School

A Day In The Life Of A Tiger

The sun beamed down onto the jungle where a tiger was about to catch a deer, when he suddenly heard a gunshot. Birds flew up into the sky, startled by the loud bang, and at that point the deer ran off too. The tiger was very curious and knew there was trouble approaching. Suddenly, five poachers appeared out of the blue and as fast as a bullet, the tiger sped off into the deep cover of the jungle, with the bloodthirsty poachers chasing him.

The tiger was sprinting rapidly like a steam train, but a few moments later he stopped to gasp for breath. This was very unwise though, because the poachers had now caught up with him. They slowly grabbed their guns, motionless and weak. The tiger just stood in one spot. A dart fired from the gun, the tiger's life flashed before its eyes, *Thud!* The tiger fell to the ground . . .

The tiger woke up, it wasn't dead but it was in this strange land, behind bars with funny people who wore strange clothes. Meanwhile, a round, fat man with a huge whip walked up to the tiger with a very sly look on his face. The tiger's heart pounded with fear, would he ever survive? Would he ever see the jungle he once roamed? He just didn't know.

Jack Banks (11)
Town Farm Primary School

A DAY IN THE LIFE OF A GUINEA PIG

'This is the life,' I squealed as I yawned and stretched, 'what are we doing today?' I plodded across to the entrance and I walked through to eat my breakfast. 'Mmm . . . yum, carrots, lettuce and parsley,' I tucked in greedily, making sure every crumb was gone. Oh look, there's our owner coming, she's going to put us on the grass. Even more food!

Our owner lifted us up gently and put us on the grass. Squeak (my best mate) sensed something. He could hear a high-pitched squawk sound coming from above. He was terrified. Suddenly a huge, black figure swooped down to attack us. I ran as fast as my little legs could carry me. Unfortunately I was pecked, I was in awful pain. Straight away my owner flew out of the door and picked us up. We were put in a small box and taken to the vet. We hated the vet. Last time he pulled half our hair out.

The vet checked us out and put this cone-thing on my head. It was so embarrassing. I went as red as a beetroot.

Our owner put us on the grass when we got home. The crow came down again. A shiver shot down my spine. I went to go and hide in the bushes when . . . the crow flew off. I had scared it away. I held my large tummy and chuckled with joy. That is the end of my adventurous, sunny Sunday. I cast my mind back to the events of today, a day 6that we will never forget!

Shauna Giddens (10)
Town Farm Primary School

A DAY IN THE LIFE OF MATT THE MOUSE

'We're starving,' my family shouted as their tummies grumbled. I could spy the chunky cheese on the table-top. I would just run and get it if it wasn't for Toby the top cat and all the mousetraps. I always get away from Toby (the stupid cat) by hiding in the cupboard. As time passed I climbed up the table leg and stared around looking for Toby. He couldn't be seen.

The cheese was on the table top just a few metres from me. 'Miaow.' Toby came running in chasing after me. I slid down the table leg, ran around the chair, hid behind the plates and grabbed the cheese. Toby blocked the mousehole and I couldn't get through. I jumped out of the window and onto the grass. The water from the sprinkler was splashing on my hair back, hurting it. I climbed up the clogged drainpipe and went through the hole in the roof and into the attic. I went down my secret hole and I skipped past all the mousetraps. My goal was in sight . . . but then I dropped the cheese through another secret hole and it bounced down by Toby. I climbed down the fireplace, grabbed the cheese and ran as fast as my legs would carry me.

As my family ate the cheese, I realised that being a mouse is a lot harder than a human's life and I will remember this day for years to come.

Danny Hadley (11)
Town Farm Primary School

A Day In The Life Of A Cat

'Da, da, da, da,' I sang as I skipped merrily down the stairs. It was a day like any other (so I thought) and the sun was beaming down onto the kitchen table. As I walked into the kitchen, my mum said in a friendly way, 'Good morning.'

'Good morning,' I replied. I poured myself a bowl of breakfast cereal and I could hear the cat meowing.

The cat walked into the kitchen and started to miaow again. As I was walking out of the kitchen I thought I heard the cat speak. I thought I heard him say, 'I want my food.' As I turned around Taz (the cat) said, 'I want my food, give me my food.' What happened next I don't know I think I . . . I fainted.

When I woke up I told my mum and dad all about it. They told me that they knew that the cat could speak and they also said that they were half witches. I was shocked and I thought it was all a dream but when I pinched myself nothing happened.

It took a while for it to kick in but I realised that this will be a day I will remember forever.

Jack Woods (11)
Town Farm Primary School

A DAY IN THE LIFE OF RONNY THE RATTLESNAKE

It was a day like any other (Ronny thought). He was chasing his breakfast, (the desert rate) when it scurried through a narrow cactus. Hungry Ronny wasn't thinking and tried to take the rat's route . . . Ronny was stuck. He was trapped between the bottom of the cactus and the hot desert ground. Ronny felt a tug at his tail. Ronny was out of his trapped position and in a box as quick as a flash.

Ronny was trapped in this metal box for an hour (roughly). Eventually when the box opened, Ronny found himself in an African safari. Ronny was searching for an escape route when he saw a poster, it said in bold, 'Rare Rattlesnake! £1,000,000 Reward'.

Ronny realised he was wanted for money. He slithered speedily towards where he started his journey. He found an open gate. Taking his chances, he crept out the gate and slithered for the desert. After hours of being on the run, Ronny reached his family habitat. Ronny rested.

A few minutes later, Ronny heard a car approach the desert. A tall, muscular man stepped out of the car. He walked carefully towards Ronny. Ronny realised someone was close to him and was ready for a venomous sting.

This man picked up Ronny, but Ronny swung his tail for the man's left leg. The man dropped him, screamed and hopped off as fast as one leg could go. Ronny was ready. Would they ever come back for the £1,000,00 rattlesnake?

Zahid Zafar (11)
Town Farm Primary School

A Day In The Life Of A Mouse

'Pass me that box,' the new house owner shouted, 'I want to start unpacking it.' I heard this and I knew that this must be the day where I might meet someone new. The hole that I was living in was very large for me, but I like them big so I have room to explore. I poked my head out of the small opening to see if I could see anyone. I did, she was a huge giant; all of a sudden she put this cat's basket in front of my door, blocking my exit.

'What am I going to do?' I was asking myself as I tried pushing the basket really hard. 'How am I going to get my food?' I got my bed and my chest of drawers and put them in front of the basket and threw myself into the drawers. The cat's basket was moved slightly by this, I was free. I got out of he hole and walked in front of the basket. 'Ahh!' I shouted, a huge ginger cat was there. I ran back into the hole. The cat's eye peeked slyly through my door. He started licking his lips. Then he went away obviously bored. I glanced behind the basket and the cat wasn't there. I tiptoed out of the hole.

I started running over to the big boxes and peering over to see if the cat was there. He wasn't I ran over to the box that said 'Food'. My mouth started watering. I jumped into the box and found some yummy cheese. I held it in my hands and sprinted back to the hole. As I nibbled my cheese I cast my mind back to the event of today I realised that I would remember this day for years to come and I would be wary of the new cat!

Lisa Stevens (11)
Town Farm Primary School

A Day In The Life Of A Toothbrush

Out of the box and taken home by a woman, the packing looks clear. I can't see many lights because they're too bright. I'm thrown into a plastic bag, feel trapped. Rattling in a car with shampoo bottles. A kid runs up the stairs with me in his hand and starts ripping my coating.

The lights are dim, the kid puts cold toothpaste on me and I go into a mouth with lots of fillings and food particles stuck. Yehh! Teeth have mouldy food stuck between steel bars (braces).

Poof! This kid must have never brushed his teeth, what bad breath he's got, oh God, his teeth are cracked and chipped and I can see holes in them. Yeh, there's worms crawling inside them. Yuck! I want to get out, get me out!

At last I am out of the black hole; he puts me in a cup with lots of brushes staring at me. Scary! I meet a nice pink brush, she's kinda good-looking, and I panic and sweat. The whole room is dark and smelly, I wonder what room it is? I am taken out of the cup and into the mouth with chewed sweets.

Bang! Felt a tap. I am soaking wet, my stick-like body smells what could've caused this smell? The water looks yellowy and big brown logs are floating around me (falls into the toilet, stays there forever). Oh no, I am trapped in the toilet forever. Help! Help!

Roya Salim (12)
Whitefriars First And Middle School

A DAY IN THE LIFE OF CROOKSHANKS

I was roaming around outside in the Quidditch Pitch when I saw the thing. The big, black dog wandering towards me. I had no idea what to do. I was scared to death when he asked me to follow him. For some reason I did and I found out 'The terrible truth'.

The dog was none other than Sirius Black! But he told me his story and I believed him. There was something about his eyes. And it takes a big spell to confound a cat so it was no spell!

Sirius said that Ron's rat - Scabbers - is the killer of Harry Potter's parents! I knew there was something wrong with that rat from the beginning. I've been trying to talk to it, but he just runs off.

Sirius's plan is to get me to steal the week's passwords from Neville so he can sneak in and rat-nap Scabbers (the rat).

I really hope this works because I hate Scabbers, as much as I'd love to eat him, I can't help wondering how Ron will feel when he finds out Scabbers is gone.

Riddhi Vyas (12)
Whitefriars First And Middle School

A Day In The Life Of Sniffles The Hamster

Hi! I'm Sniffles the hamster. It's twelve at night, it's my playtime because I'm nocturnal. I'm just going to have some fun running around my cage, see you in the morning.

It's about 8.00am. I'm going to go to sleep now. Bang! My cage door just opened, in comes a hand 'sniff' it's Mum, she wants a cuddle. After she puts me back, I nestle in my house.

Later the door closes - Mum leaving for school - thank goodness. I drift back off. Then my cage gets lifted by Nan to go back in Mum's room (I have to go downstairs then they sleep).

I go to sleep for about half an hour, then I wake from another door slamming - Nan going to work - maybe I'll get some sleee . . . . Nope, here comes the usual panting noise of Cassie the dog, she's come to stare at me again, great!

It's now quarter to four, Mum comes upstairs, shoos Cassie out for another cuddle. I get some sleep then I wake up on the ride downstairs. Mum's obviously going to get a good night's sleep, she goes off to bed.

Now in the front room with Nan and Grandad watching TV. Bang! I have a cuddle with Nan then they go off to bed.

No sleep all day and now it's time for fun. I think I'll catch up on some sleep instead, after a run!

Katie Billington (12)
Whitefriars First And Middle School

A Day In The Life Of An Angel

Entry No 1
Date   2nd June 2003
Time   8.15pm
Subject Being dead!

Guess what? I'm dead!
Can you believe it, I mean one minute I'm alive and breathing and the next I'm being placed into the cold, dark ground. Being dead isn't that bad, actually it's quite fun being an angel because I'm unique, I don't have to go and change my clothes I just think of what I want to wear and I'm wearing it.

Entry No 2
Date   3rd June 2003
Time   6.30pm
Subject The Old People's Home

Today was wicked! I went to the old people's home to scare a few people. I thought I'd only scare about two or three people but it turned out the whole elderly people's home got spooked to bits.

Entry No 3
Date   4th June 2003
Time   9.35pm
Subject Telling people about being dead is hard

I just told Afsaneh; my best mate that I was an angel and she was so upset because she just found out I had died. She went to America to see her family. She didn't even make it to my funeral.

Entry No 4
Date   5th June 2003
Time   11.30pm
Subject Just hanging out with my best mate at the Mall

Today was great, we went to the Mall to do some shopping for Afsaneh because she needs some new outfits. Oh and guess what happened at the Mall? Everybody though Afsaneh was mad because she was talking to me and I'm invisible.

Entry No 5
Date   6th June 2003
Time   12.30pm
Subject   Am I really supposed to be dead

Something really dumb just happened. The Angel of Death just told me I wasn't supposed to be dead until another 70 years. What a big misunderstanding.

Entry No 6
Date   7th June 2003
Time   1.30pm
Subject   Back to being human

I miss my life as an angel, I want to go back but I don't want to leave my life. Oh well, I've got to face the fact that I'm not going to die until another 70 years.

Anyway, it was great being an angel!

Mamuna Qureshi (11)
Whitefriars First And Middle School

A Day In The Life Of Little Orphan Annie

'We love you Miss Hannigan.'
'Hi there, my name is Annie and I live here at Miss Hannigan's orphanage.

Life is horrible here, we have to do all the work and are only fed mush. If we are naughty or won't do any work, Miss Hannigan locks us in the paddle closet. I would know as I have been in there a few times.

When I escaped, I found a dog that I called Sandy. Miss Hannigan doesn't know about him yet. If she found out about him, he would be sent to the Sausage Factory.

'Kill, kill.' There she goes again. If she hears talking, we have to get up and start cleaning straight away. We have to wear old rags and never get new clothes. We never have nice things to eat at all. Sometimes we get hot mush, but when Miss Hannigan is in a bad mood we have to eat it cold.

If ever we have visitors, we are treated nice and look like we have a nice life. Miss Hannigan's favourite sayings are 'Kill, kill', 'My little pig's droppings', 'Rotten orphans' and her newest one 'You'll stay up till this dump shines like the top of the Chrysler building'. Because no one loves her, we have to tell her that we do.

Well, I got to go now, as she will probably want me to clean up for her. Bye.

Georgie Adams (12)
Whitefriars First And Middle School

A DAY IN THE LIFE OF BARRY

A day in the life of Barry starts off with him having a grumpy
mood and trying to have a fight with his little sister, me.
Then straight after he has breakfast,
to everyone's joy he gets ready for school and went.

On the way to school he knocked for some of his mates.
So him and his mates got to school and as usual they were late
so they had to go to the office and get a late
stamp in his diary. Then when he had got the late stamp he
had to go to his first lesson, which was English with Mr Byrne,
which Barry doesn't particularly like! He got sent out for
talking. He was walking down the corridor, when his head of year saw
him and said, 'First of all, you have trainers on,
second of all, what's wrong with your hair and last of all, why has
Mr Byrne sent you out?'
'Mr Byrne doesn't like me, my hair's OK and my shoes are at home.'
Barry said in an argumentative way.
'Barry, go to detention at lunchtime.'
But when lunchtime came Barry obviously didn't go but when
3.30 came along he saw his head of year.
'Why didn't you come, I haven't got time for explanations
just come tomorrow.'
So Barry just went home and because he was so tired,
he went to bed.

Kellie Smith (12)
Whitefriars First And Middle School

LEEDS UNITED - MARCHING ON TOGETHER

My name is Harry Kewell. I'm going to tell you about the days I play in the Champion's League Final.

The whole team's alarm clock rang and rang. I got up, then the whole team got up. Some had a bath and some of us had a shower but I had a bath. After the bath we had some breakfast. Then we got our bags ready for the big game. As I had breakfast as I was too nervous to eat it all up. The coach came, we put our bags on the coach, our manager David O'Leary had a headcount. As we got to the stadium we looked at the pitch and met the players. As I shook hands with Michael Owen a streaker ran on the pitch and the streaker shook my hand. I saw her body parts and she was on telly. As the game started I scored a goal and no one else scored a goal except for after half-time. We went into the changing rooms, the team was jumping up and down because we thought we'd won. But in the second-half, they scored two goals by Michael Owen. As it was five minutes to go I scored two goals to make it 3-2, and we won.

David Webster (12)
Whitefriars First And Middle School

A DAY IN THE LIFE OF MRS PRITCHARD

Thursday:
A day in the life of Lynne Pritchard, formally known to us as Mrs Pritchard.
She wakes up, goes downstairs and eats her breakfast. Then she goes upstairs and has a shower.
Then she brushes her teeth and dresses herself. Then she gives her daughter and husband a kiss. Then she makes her way to her car and drives to school. She gets to school, says hello to the staff in the staffroom as she gets herself a coffee to wake her up a bit more. Then she makes her way to her office and makes herself comfortable. Then the phone rings, and she answers it. It turns out to be a wrong number. Just then the bell rings for first play. She goes to the staffroom and sits there for a while, well at last the bell rings. *Riiiiiinggg!* The bell has run, she has to go to the office just in case someone is in trouble and has to see her. Surprisingly no one comes, she is happy about it, in fact she is so happy that she mentions this in assembly and instead of getting two playtimes we got five playtimes. But not for today, for Friday.

Anyway, usually we get Mrs Pritchard after lunchtime and we do art, history or geography. Today we are doing art and there is a person from whom we are copying drawings from and he is famous but dead, his name is Escher. So we do that for two hours and then Mrs Pritchard plays a game with us for 30 minutes then the bell goes and we go home.

Mrs Pritchard goes to the staffroom and marks our work, which is our class 7D. Then she has a cup of tea and goes into her car and goes home to her husband and daughter.

Rhonda Black (12)
Whitefriars First And Middle School

A DAY IN THE LIFE OF JIMMY FLOYD HASSELBAINK

Jimmy wakes up at 7.30 because he has football training and a big football match against West Ham, tonight at Upton Park. Jimmy comes downstairs to have something to eat before he goes football training at 11.30, some bacon rolls. Jimmy gets his football boots and his other training gear in the car. He arrives at the training at 11.00 to get changed, has a chat to the manager about tonight's game. He finishes training at 2.00, gets changed, the players get on the coach and go to Upton Park for tonight's game. When the players arrive at West Ham they go to an Italian restaurant and Hasselbaink has some pasta and salad. The game is in five minutes and both sets of players are ready to play the game. It's the end of the first half and it is 2-0 to Chelsea, Hasselbaink scored one of the goals and Zola got the other. It's the end of the game and Chelsea won 2-0. It's Chelsea's first away win this season, Hasselbaink gets Man of the Match. He and the players go home and go to sleep.

Ben Cleary (12)
Whitefriars First And Middle School

A DAY IN THE LIFE OF A . . . DOG

I woke from the fireplace, I walked towards the mirror. Suddenly I gasped in horror at what I saw. I saw a waggly tail with my tongue sticking out. I heard someone coming towards the door. Just then I got the urge to shout and the words that came out were 'Woof, woof,' and then a pile of papers came through a big hole in the door. I jumped because I heard some voices. As it came closer I heard
'Blah, blah, blah.'
I couldn't understand a word those animals were saying. They were at each other like me and that whisker-faced toerag next door. She is really irritating. I could kill her. Her name is Muffy, stupid little thing. It was midday and I heard my name being called. I ran towards the caller. There by the door I saw a plate of food which had a piece of chicken and a weird thing sitting beside it. It looked weird but I decided to eat it anyway. Then I wanted to go for a walk. I just about fitted through the cat flap. Why do they call it a cat flap? They should call it a waggle tail thing flap. Then I saw a plate of food at the door of a shop. I took the food and I ran. I finally found my way back and went to sleep and whispered to myself, 'Sweet dreams.'

Vaishali Patel (11)
Whitefriars First And Middle School

A Day In The Life Of A T-Rex

'Why do those blasted aerodactyls have to wake me up at 7.30 in the morning? Can't a dinosaur get any sleep around here?' I thought in my head.

At that moment my partner woke up, a beautiful thing she is.

'I'm feeling kind of hungry,' I said to my partner.

'I've already caught some compy darling,' said my partner.

But about thirty seconds later, I saw the eggs hatching. My partner and I were both shocked and excited. I felt so tense, I just wanted them to hatch and at last they did. We called them Bubbles, Herbert, Dilly and Billy.

I felt so happy at that moment, I couldn't express it.

'Do you think the babies are hungry yet?' I asked/

'Yeah, I think they need to be fed now.'

My wife and I went over to our babies and we were shocked by what we saw.

'Leave Bubbles alone,' I shouted out.

But it was too late. That damned triceratops ate Bubbles. Now that coward was running. I was going to get that sadistic dinosaur if it was the last thing I did.

'Come out, come out, you coward,' I shouted out.

Two hours had gone and I still couldn't find him.

I still can't believe I didn't find that triceratops. He's one lucky dinosaur.

'Help me, help me someone, anyone.'

'Who said that?' I shouted out. Then I saw it, a baby triceratops drowning in the river. I didn't know whether to save it or let it drown. I decided to save it. I jumped into the water and told it to get on my back. After it had thanked me I went back to my partner and babies and told them of my doings. She wasn't happy but I knew I did the right thing.

Jason McKenzie (12)
Whitefriars First And Middle School

A DAY IN THE LIFE OF A VICTORIAN SERVANT NAMED SUSAN BAKER

11/5/1872

Today I reluctantly woke up at 6 o'clock. I hurriedly put on my maid's dress and ran into the kitchen. Cook was already making the breakfast , so I quickly went to help her.
'Susan, you're late!' snapped the cook, looking more disgruntled than ever.
'S-sorry ma'am,' I stuttered.
'Make haste!' she shouted.
I took some bread by the fire to toast. I had just done it perfectly when a cry made me jump and knock the bread on the floor, as I ran to the children's room, where a sight of disarray met my eyes.

Charlotte, Victor and baby Igor were wailing their heads off, in the middle of the nursery. By the time I had hushed them up, it was time for breakfast.

I took the tray of mouth-watering food to the family. After breakfast, I took the children for a walk. There I had a moment's peace while they played. When I told them we had to go home, surprisingly they quietly walked back to me. I could tell they were plotting something.

Indoors, I ravenously had some leftovers to eat. The family ate lunch while I cleaned all the rooms.

After lunch the children had a nap, while I helped Cook prepare dinner. Then I remembered, what were the children plotting?

Dinner time came and the family sat down to eat. I had leftovers. Afterwards, the family relaxed. I went up to my room. As I got into bed, leaves and mud squelched around my feet. Those children! Sometimes I wonder, is it really worth it?

Nikita Patel (12)
Whitefriars First And Middle School

A Day In The Life Of Arsenal And The Cup Final

My name is Thierry Henry and I'm going to tell you about the day which I will not forget. The whole team woke up including me in our posh hotel in Wales thinking of that special day. We got our bags ready and went downstairs for breakfast. Some of the team members couldn't even eat, as they were too nervous. Once we finished our breakfast we stood outside waiting for the coach to arrive. When it arrived the bags were put in the boot and we stepped inside the coach. The manager, Arsene Wenger, counted all the members of the team to make sure none of us was left behind. We were nearly there when the fans were standing and waving for their team. When we got to the stadium, we got off the coach and walked through the tunnel onto the pitch where we looked at the pitch and said hello to our opponents. When we went into the changing room afterwards, we talked about this big occasion, especially me. It was that time. I was trembling, we walked onto the pitch. The crowd shouted and waited for the kick-off. The whistle blew, chances were made when suddenly Frederic Ljunberg scored. That gave us hope, only for so long, as in the second half Michael Owen scored two goals to give Liverpool the lead. The whistle blew, it was over. We lost our chance to win the FA Cup. Oh well, we will try again next year.

Sean Prudden (12)
Whitefriars First And Middle School

A DAY IN THE LIFE OF A PENCIL

'Ouch!' I said as I was picked up from the floor by John in the morning. John is so rough with me. My old master was much better. Oh how I miss my old master, Master Paul. But now my master is John. Oh I do wish I could be back with Master Paul but I'm not sure I can.

You're probably wondering how I got to be with Master John. Well, I was resting in Master Paul's pencil case when all of a sudden Master John pulled me out and scraped a little patch of me and wrote his name on it. Paul tried to get me back but he couldn't. John wouldn't give me to Paul.

Master John was fiddling around with me and he dropped me. Ooh how painful when my lead broke. It nearly killed me. But after that he didn't pick me up. He kicked me under a cupboard. It was horrible and dark. I met a sharpener and he told me that he had been there for a long time and that I wouldn't get out for a while.

Suddenly somebody picked me up. It was a young child and she put me in her mouth and she made me all soggy. Then she said I wasn't sharp and she sharpened me. I screeched in pain. It was like someone sticking daggers into my back. I went smaller until I couldn't breathe then I luckily was put back into Paul's pencil case. Yippee.

Leena Patel (12)
Whitefriars First And Middle School

A DAY IN THE LIFE OF BRITNEY SPEARS

'I don't want to do this line! Get me a Coke now!'

'Yes, Madam.'

'Madam you have mail.'

'Well, give it to me, then. Huh! Where's my Coke. Hurry up now! Right, when I go on Top Of The Pops I want a dress worth one million pounds. Where's my Coke? God, you people are so slow. I don't know why I hired you. If you don't let me do this line I will fire you, understand?'

'Yes, yes madam.'

'Right I want to do my line now. Ready, 1, 2, 3, hit it. Hit me baby one more time.'

'Right, well done Britney, time to go home now.'

'Home? I have not even had my Coke yet and I am getting very angry with you!'

'Here Madam, here's your Coke!'

'About time, right I am going home now. See you on Wednesday and one more thing, don't be thick-skulled again and do what I tell you to!'

'OK Madam, see you on Wednesday.'

'Yes, see you on Wednesday! Driver take me home and step on it.'

'Yes of course Madam.'

'Thank you, driver, see you soon! Huh, I am so tired. Mum! You won't believe the day I've had. All the people that I have are so idiotic. I had to wait twenty minutes for my Coke! Can you believe it?'

'Oh dear, Sweetie, what do you want for dinner?'

'It's late Mum so I am going to go to bed! See you early in the morning!'

'Yes Darling, night night.'

Natasha McPhillips (12)
Whitefriars First And Middle School

A Day In The Life Of A Tree

I lived in a large wood. It was autumn and my leaves had turned orange.

One morning I woke up to birds twittering on my branches. A woodpecker was making a hole in my trunk looking for insects.

Suddenly I heard shouting and some children came running up and started swinging on my branches and breaking them off. A voice called out and the children ran off.

Two teenagers came from behind a bush. I felt a pain as a knife was dug into me as they carved their names.

During the afternoon a wind started blowing and my leaves started falling to the ground in a heap.

A dog came up and started scratching at my bark. Later on I heard a sound. From a distance it sounded like a blade. It was coming closer and closer and getting louder and louder. I saw the tree next to me trembling with fear. It began to shake, rattle and roll until it came crashing to the ground.

It was now my turn but the man with the big saw said
'That's enough for today.'
Phew I get to live another day.

I heard a lot of noise in the night. A bear came and started to dig a hole in me and it lay there. Then I heard thunder and lightning and it was pouring with acid rain. I was on fire.

Shane Maisey (12)
Whitefriars First And Middle School

A DAY IN THE LIFE OF A DOG

Hello, my name is Cassie and I am a black standard poodle. I usually get up at about 7 o'clock in the morning when my owners get up to make a cup of tea. I have a biscuit with them and then I go downstairs and sleep on the settee until everyone has got up. I bark quite loudly so that they will let me out in the garden for a sniff around. Suddenly the house is quiet and I am left on my own so I decide to have another sleep.

Later in the morning one of my owners comes home. I greet her by jumping up and wagging my tail. I can see that she has been shopping and hope that she has bought me some food. I know that it is getting near time for my walk so I follow her around the house just waiting for her to say the words, 'Shall we go to the woods for a walk, Cassie?'

When the time for a walk comes around I get very excited and race around the house waiting for my lead to be put on. Then we go out of the house and go to the woods. I love it in the woods, there are lots of different smells and I can run about as much as I want. I don't like it when it rains though. I hate getting wet because when I get home I have to be dried with the towel and sometimes with the hairdryer as well. Sometimes in the woods I see other dogs. Some are nice and some are not. Sometimes they chase me and I get very frightened and run to my owners to save me from them.

One day when we got back home I saw a cat and I love chasing cats. The cat disappeared and I had run a long way from my house chasing it and I couldn't find my way back home. I came to the seaside and I did something that I shouldn't have done. I went into the sea and did doggy paddle. I didn't like it because I don't like getting wet. I kept on swimming but I couldn't swim to the shore. Then I saw some people in a boat near me so I tried to swim to them. They spotted me and helped me get on the boat. They took me to their house and looked on my collar and saw a telephone number so they rang it and my owners came to collect me later.

When I got back home it was my teatime. I was very hungry so I ate very quickly. Everybody had come home by this time. After tea I barked to go out into the garden. I was very happy to come home again. Later on my owners decided to go to bed. I usually wait for them to say it's bedtime and then I go upstairs and into my basket and go to sleep. I was very tired after my adventure.

Hayley Shelton (9)
Woodside County Middle School

A DAY IN THE LIFE OF WILLOW WAGGER
(Based on a true story)

My name is Willow but my family call me Wagger and I am the luckiest dog alive. I will tell you why.

At the beginning of my life I lived here and there but nowhere special and, finally, after being ill-treated by some gypsies, I was rescued by a dog warden and taken to a dog rescue centre and I thought my life of eighteen months was over until two weeks later.

It was just another day in my kennel when suddenly the kennel maid came and got me. At first I thought I was going for a walk but to my surprise we went the other way to reception and there was a family there. I liked the look of them especially the one called Mummy (anyway that's what the little girl called her). She talked nicely to me and took me for a walk with the daddy and the little girl. Inside I was saying, 'Please take me home with you,' when to my surprise the daddy said, 'Willow, would you like to come home with us?'
I said *'Woof, woof,'* which means yes in dog language. I just could not believe my lucky paws. Now I've been with them two great years. I am spoiled rotten. This is my day.

I get up when my new mummy gets up and she takes me to do what a dog's got to do and then I have breakfast and go with Mummy to take the girl to school. Then I just laze around the house and sleep, play, eat and have lots of fuss made of me until bedtime when my daddy takes me for my last walk.

These have been the best days of my life and I want to stay with my new family for ever.

Gemma Thornley (9)
Woodside County Middle School

A DAY IN THE LIFE OF A GAZELLE

The first thing I had to do today was to catch up with the rest of the herd because I had overslept.

The first thing we do every morning is go to the waterhole for a drink. While I was there I thought I saw a predator stalking us, but I didn't mind because I was in a herd. Then we moved along saying goodbye to our animal friends. I was last again. (Oh did I mention I was the youngest in the herd?)

When I had caught up, we went over to the plains to eat some grass. (I don't particularly like it, but my mum says if I don't eat it, I won't be a big strong gazelle.)

Suddenly, out of nowhere, a lion leapt out, pouncing! It narrowly missed me, but it did get another old gazelle. I started running as fast as I could but I was still in the tail-enders of the herd. Luckily, soon after we had started running it gave up and went away.

By now, it was quite dark and our herd decided to go back to the waterhole to have a last drink and then go and sleep somewhere.

We took a quick drink and also a quiet retreat, just in case any trouble sprung up (I wasn't last this time.) When we found a good place to sleep in, my mum sent me straight to bed.

Sam Dickinson (10)
Woodside County Middle School

A DAY IN THE LIFE OF AN ANT

One bright and sunny morning there was a black ant colony working hard. There was one ant in particular. His name was Antony and he was about three months old. I'm going to tell you about one day in his life, an exciting day.

It all started on a summer's morning. Antony was playing outside with his friends. Unfortunately he was in a child's garden. The giant found Antony and picked him up and put him in a glass jar. Poor Antony was scared stiff. He just sat there, I mean wouldn't you be scared if you were picked up by a giant, nearly squashed and stuffed into a jar?

The giant took him inside, onto the table and glared at him with giant eyeballs. Suddenly he heard a call saying
'Dinner's ready!'
It sounded like a trumpet! The giant ran to the kitchen. Suddenly the giant tripped over a shoe. He fell over and banged onto the table and the glass jar I was in fell down and was smashed. I ran as fast as my six legs could take me.
'I'm, free, I'm free,' he chanted.

So that is his exciting day.

Rebecca Ponnuthurai (10)
Woodside County Middle School